Flirting
with
Disaster

ALSO BY RHONDA STAPLETON

Stupid Cupid

Flirting

with

Disaster

Rhonda Stapleton

SIMON PULSE
New York   London   Toronto   Sydney

SIMON PULSE
An imprint of Simon & Schuster Children's Publishing Division
1230 Avenue of the Americas, New York, NY 10020
First Simon Pulse paperback edition March 2010
Copyright © 2010 by Rhonda Stapleton
All rights reserved, including the right of reproduction in whole or in part in any form.
SIMON PULSE and colophon are registered trademarks of Simon & Schuster, Inc.

For information about special discounts for bulk purchases, please contact
Simon & Schuster Special Sales at 1-866-506-1949 or business@simonandschuster.com.
The Simon & Schuster Speakers Bureau can bring authors to your live event. For more
information or to book an event contact the Simon & Schuster Speakers Bureau
at 1-866-248-3049 or visit our website at www.simonspeakers.com.
Designed by Paul Weil
The text of this book was set in Adobe Caslon Pro.
Manufactured in the United States of America
2 4 6 8 10 9 7 5 3 1
Library of Congress Control Number 2009927788
ISBN 978-1-4169-7465-9
ISBN 978-1-4169-9907-2 (eBook)

This is dedicated to my parents, Pat and Ron, for supporting me through all those rough patches in my life, and for showing me what true strength is. You guys made me the person I am today. Okay, that came out a lot scarier-sounding than I meant. Haha.

This is also dedicated to my sister, Lisa Lisa and the Strawberry Jam, who has the magical ability to trip over grass, who sprayed my entire wardrobe with stinky rose perfume after I shoved an onion under her nose, and who always makes me giggle until I get hiccups. You're still pretty!

Acknowledgments

First, I'd like to give a huge, huuuuge thank you to Bryan Jones, and my kids, Shelby and Bryan, for your help, inspiration, and patience. You guys are the cornerstone of my life, and you make me happy every day.

Thanks to my parents, Pat and Ron; my sister, Lisa; Forrest and Lynne Jones; my cousin Jody; and my aunt Lou. And also, a big shout-out to all the Stapletons and Stevens in West Virginia—I love you guys!

Thanks to all my friends—there are way too many of you to list, but you guys know who you are. You've been there for me through thick and thin. Thank you.

Caryn, my awesome agent, thank you for being so great to work with. You rock. I look forward to working on many more books with you.

Anica and Mike, my two incredible editors, I couldn't have done these books without you guys. Anica, I adore my '80s New Kids on the Block postcard and keep it by my desk for daily inspiration. Mike, you killed me in the dance-off with your awesome robot moves. We're not worthy!

I'd like to thank all of Simon Pulse—my copyeditors, cover artist, marketing team, publicity, etc. You guys are so fun and fabulous to work with, and you've really made me feel like a first-class star.

And last but not least, I want to thank YOU, the totally cool and obviously intelligent reader who has picked up my story. Shine on, you crazy diamond.

Chapter 1

"There are lots of fun ways to have a good time at a party without drinking!" Mrs. Cahill, our health class teacher, hopped up on the end of her large desk. She crossed her legs beneath a flowing brown paisley skirt.

A few people chuckled at her words, and I bit back a laugh myself. At least she was enthusiastic about her topic. It was hard for me to scrape up enthusiasm for anything on a Monday, but Mrs. Cahill never lacked any.

"So, what did you guys list?" Mrs. Cahill asked. "Let's share a few of our choices with the class. Now as I said before, I won't be collecting them. This is for you to take home and hopefully implement in your life to encourage a lifestyle that avoids alcohol."

Yeah, right. I was sure most of my classmates would instantly give up partying because of a list made in health class. That was *totally* plausible.

I glanced down at my paper. Our in-class assignment was to write ten "fun" things to do that didn't involve alcohol. Out of my ten items, six of them involved staring longingly at Derek, the guy I've been madly in love with since freshman year. No way was I going to say that out loud, though.

James Powers thrust his hand into the air, a smarmy grin on his face.

"Go ahead, James," Mrs. Cahill said. "What did you write?"

He made a big show of holding up his paper in front of his face. "Ahem. I put, 'have sex.'"

His buddies around him guffawed, and several girls tittered behind their hands. I rolled my eyes. Mrs. Cahill should have known better than to call on James.

"Oh my God, James!" one girl whispered, giggling. "You're so crazy."

Mrs. Cahill blushed and pressed a hand to her beet-red cheeks. "Well, that's . . . not quite what I meant."

Mallory Robinson, my mortal enemy and the bane of my

existence, turned and whispered something to her friends, Jordan and Carrie. Jordan nodded briefly in response, but Carrie barely looked at her. They both turned their attention back to James. Mallory's face fell. She quickly recovered and started writing in her notebook.

I smirked. The dynamics between Mallory and her friends had changed ever since I'd set her up last month with Bobby Loward, a.k.a. Bobby Blowhard, the biggest weenie I'd ever known. It was still the most talked-about love match around school, even though the magic had worn off and Mallory and Bobby had split up a few weeks ago.

Of course, nobody else knew that there'd been magic involved in their hookup, let alone that I was the cupid responsible for the match. Total secrecy was the first rule of my job at Cupid's Hollow. I wasn't allowed to tell a soul that my hot-pink PDA was used to matchmake my classmates using the latest in handheld technology—love arrows shot through e-mail.

Not that anyone would believe me if I *were* allowed to spill the beans. Though maybe the ridiculous pairing of Mallory and Bobby Blowhard would be convincing proof.

Mallory's friends hadn't treated her the same since. It didn't matter that they'd broken up the day the spell wore off. The damage was already done.

My only regret was that I couldn't step forward and claim credit for what was surely an act of humanity: keeping Mallory's stuck-up nose out of my best friend Maya Takahashi's dating life by giving Mallory a relationship of her own to focus on. But the cupid contract I'd signed meant I couldn't spill the beans—and frankly, I feared my boss Janet too much to screw around with that.

"What about spin the bottle, then?" Mitzi, one of the flaky chicks in our class, asked. "That's just making out, not actually *doing* it."

Andy Carsen, my other best friend, bit back a laugh. She leaned over and whispered to me, "I think the whole point of the exercise was to *avoid* bottles."

"No kidding," I said quietly, shaking my head.

Mrs. Cahill looked over at me. "Felicity, since you feel like talking, do you have anything to add to our conversation? What did you write down on your list?"

Whoops. I glanced at my paper, reading aloud an entry that wouldn't totally humiliate me for life. "Um, play poker."

Not that I knew how to play, but I don't think that mattered to her. At least I didn't say something that involved being naked.

"Good answer!" Mrs. Cahill beamed at me. "Card games are a fun and healthy alternative to drinking at a party."

"What an ass kisser," I heard Mallory whisper to her friends. They giggled.

Andy spun around in her seat and stared hard at Mallory until she looked away.

The bell rang, dismissing us from class.

"Make sure you hold on to those lists," Mrs. Cahill said loudly over the bell as we all rushed to evacuate. "Especially since we're nearing prom season."

"Thank *God* that's over," I said to Andy as we walked down the hall. "I swear, that class gets weirder every day."

"No kidding," Andy said. "I don't think Mrs. Cahill was expecting those responses. She should know James by now, though. He's always going to give the most obnoxious answers he can think of."

"You know, I'd feel bad for her if she hadn't given us this dumb assignment in the first place."

I hated health class with the fiery passion of a thousand burning suns. It was possibly the most boring, ineffective course I'd taken to date. The only good thing about it was I didn't have to take gym anymore, one of the other most terrible classes ever.

I was so not athletic, and it was highly unfair that I was forced to participate in events that made me look like a dumbass. Ever see me dribble a basketball? Once you did, you'd understand my plight.

But health class was not much better. For one period every day I was trapped in a room with both James and Bobby. And even worse, with Mallory, who took every opportunity to shoot me nasty glares across the room, or make snotty comments to her friends.

In between shooting me the evil eye, Mallory would sneak peeks at James, who was her boyfriend freshman year. She was probably wondering why they weren't still together. Um, maybe because she was a total cow. Not that James even noticed her anymore. He was too busy trying to show the whole class how very funny he was.

Fortunately, Andy was in there with me. She helped make the time go faster with her dry humor.

"Hey, Felicity, that was a good answer," Bobby Blowhard said, appearing out of nowhere and sliding in between me and Andy. "I didn't know you played poker. What's your favorite kind? I like Texas Hold'em."

Fortunately for us, and all of mankind, Bobby wasn't wearing his usual mesh workout shirt. Instead he had on a tight black spandex top. I suppose it was his way of enticing people to look at his muscles, but I can't say it worked on me.

"Actually, I don't really play," I mumbled, trying not to be rude, but also not wanting to encourage him into further conversation.

Bobby was . . . overbearing, to say the least. I'd noticed that once the cupid spell wore off him, he lost his attraction toward Mallory and instantly regained it toward me.

Lucky, lucky me.

"Oh." Bobby paused and flexed a little. "Well, maybe I could teach you sometime. I know lots of card games, actually, and—"

"Hey," Andy interrupted, "it's time for us to head to lunch." She grabbed my elbow and led me away.

"Okay, see ya!" Bobby bellowed to my back.

I gave him a halfhearted wave as Andy and I darted down the hall.

"I owe you," I told her gratefully. "Cokes are on me."

We headed to the cafeteria and made our way through the lunch line to our usual table, where Maya was already waiting for us. She was holding hands and talking closely with her boyfriend of almost a month, Scott Baker.

I swear, the guy looked like he had a permanent flush whenever he was around Maya. It was cute, even if it was a little goofy. But it made me happy to see her with a guy who was perfect for her.

After the fiasco of matching her up with three guys at once, I'd learned the hard way that it was much better to do a one-on-one pairing. Much, *much* better. Maya had started dating Scott after that, and they'd been going strong since. Of course, I had sent them a cupid e-mail to encourage their attraction (not that they'd needed it).

And just as cool, I'd recently received my second bonus check for a lasting love match. Score!

"Hey," Andy said, plopping down beside Maya. "How's my favorite couple today?"

"Oh, hey guys!" Maya shot us a big smile. "How are you? Anything good going on?"

"Not too much," I said. "Except in health class James said he wanted to have sex instead of drink at a party, and Mrs. Cahill about had a heart attack." I sat on Andy's other side and started noshing on my burrito.

Maya shook her head. "Yeah, that sounds like him. And more exciting than my morning."

"Actually Maya got an A on her French test," Scott interjected. "She beat all of us with the top score. She could probably teach our class and put Monsieur LeBec out of a job."

Maya shrugged, blushing. "I guess you're just a good study partner," she replied. She glanced at her watch, then stood. "Oh, I gotta go. I told Mr. Seagle I'd help him set up the chem lab today before class."

"I'll go with you," Scott said, automatically rising beside her.

"You two lovebirds have fun. Try not to coo all over each other," Andy ribbed.

Maya shot her a fake glare. "Funny, funny."

She and Scott headed out of the cafeteria, glued to each other's sides. I couldn't help but grin at the sight of them.

"If I didn't love Maya so much, I'd be super jealous," Andy said, watching them go. "She looks so happy."

I jerked my head to look at her. "Jealous? Really? I thought you'd sworn off love."

Andy bit her lower lip. She drew lines in her creamed corn with her fork. Why the school was serving creamed corn with burritos, I'd never know.

"I thought so too," she said with a sigh, "but seeing how good they are together makes me think maybe I'm missing out on something."

My heart rate kick-started to about a million beats a minute.

Andy had been on a self-imposed sabbatical from guys for a while now and hadn't shown any interest in dating. So this was the opportunity I'd been waiting for—to hear her say she was ready for me to find her a love match.

Okay, not that she knew I'd be matchmaking her, but whatever. I knew I could do the job justice. After all, Maya and Scott were still going strong, as were DeShawn and Marisa, an unlikely couple I'd paired on a whim who seemed to beat all odds and make it work. That relationship had also changed DeShawn's bad attitude, and he wasn't the überbutthead he used to be.

I just knew I could help Andy find love too.

"Yeah, Scott seems like living proof that there are nice guys out there," I said casually.

"No kidding. If only we could all be so lucky. She snagged herself a good one." Andy took a bite of her food, then shot me a pointed look. "Not that *you* won't be that lucky soon, with you-know-who."

My stomach flipped over in excitement at the thought of Derek smiling at me the way Scott smiled at Maya. God, would there ever be a time when Derek didn't make every part of me feel utterly, painfully alive? A time when I wasn't a total wreck, wishing I could get him to see me as the perfect match for him?

For the thousandth time since taking the cupid job, I rued the fact that I couldn't matchmake myself.

"Well, who knows what'll happen with that," I said, biting off a big hunk of my burrito. I chewed and swallowed before speaking again. "Our plan of me repeatedly throwing myself in front of him hasn't seemed to work yet."

Not only had Derek *not* fallen head over heels in love and dropped down on one knee to ask me out on a date, things hadn't progressed much further than the casual conversation stage we had been at for a couple of months now. It was slow torture, and yet I was putting myself willingly through it every step of the way.

"Well, maybe we'll both be surprised." Andy shot me a crooked smile. "Maybe love will strike us both out of the blue."

I grinned back. "If it can happen for Maya, it surely will happen for you."

Because I'd sure see to it that it would.

That afternoon I made it my primary mission during my classes to select the lead candidates for Andy's love match. Holding my tricked-out PDA just out of the teacher's line of vision, I flipped through the profiles I'd stored in it and found two guys I thought might suit Andy and that Maya and I might not mind having around.

First was Tyler Macintosh, a cute guy who plays drums in a local band. He's popular and always has a big crowd around him wherever he goes. His light brown, wavy hair looks casually tousled without any effort, and he's always smiling and laughing with his friends. Andy could definitely appreciate his positive attitude and enthusiasm.

The other guy was Jacob Simpson, a superhot, smart guy on the soccer team. I didn't know much else about him, other than he's really, really attractive, with big dimples in his cheeks, and black hair. Oh, and a soccer player. Duh, me. Anyway, he truly is the perfect blend of brains and brawn, and Andy tended to like a good combo of both those elements.

Yes, these were promising initial character notes, but I still needed to flesh out their profiles before I chose between them. I wanted to do right by Andy . . . and to cover my butt with Janet, my boss at Cupid's Hollow, by making sure the match would meet the minimum compatibility requirements. Luckily, I had classes with both guys, which made it easy to add notes into my LoveLine 3000.

During anthropology, while Mr. Wiley scrawled furiously

across the chalkboard, I tucked my PDA into my lap and continued enhancing the profiles I'd created of Tyler and Jacob.

Name: Tyler Macintosh

Age: 17

Interests: Loves music—carries drumsticks everywhere in back pocket. Also into performing, and likes to bang drumsticks on his desk when teacher's gone. Good sense of humor. He cracked a funny joke today about night-shift waitresses at Waffle House.

And he totally checked out Andy at lunch when she walked by. But then chewed his sandwich with mouth open. Ew! And did "seafood" to another guy. Obviously likes attention.

Style: Casual rocker

Name: Jacob Simpson

Age: 17

Interests: Sports and fashion—likes to wear soccer socks and shin guards, even when not in a game. Into fitness and has nice butt—go, Greenville High soccer hotties! Also checked out Andy at lunch. Gee, surprise.

Made crack about "large" girl in anthropology class. :-(

Style: Preppy sports guy

At the end of the day it looked like seafood and drumsticks won out over tight soccer tushie. While Jacob might have been cuter than Tyler, the fat joke he made wasn't cool. I felt bad for the butt of his joke, Justine, who'd just stared straight ahead in class and pretended not to hear him.

I shot Jacob a glare when I caught his eye, just to show I disapproved, and I made a mental note never to matchmake him to any of my friends. The jerk.

Yeah, Tyler was the no-brainer choice here. I'd seen Andy check him out once or twice before. Plus, it didn't hurt that Andy was wild about musicians. She had pictures of drummers from several bands plastered all over her notebooks.

Surely it had to be fate.

I composed my e-mail to Tyler, CC'd Andy, and sent it. When they opened the e-mails, they'd fall in love instantly, matched together for two weeks of bliss.

Awesome. I couldn't wait to see Andy happy in love.

Chapter 2

"I ran out of light blue. Can I share with you?" Derek picked up his painting and moved beside me, settling into the seat on my right.

My heart nearly stopped in my chest, and I put my paintbrush down to keep my shaking hand from dripping paint all over the art class table. "Oh, uh, of course."

I pushed the tempera paint toward Derek. We were doing monochromatic self-portraits for our newest art project, and he and I had both coincidentally chosen the color blue to paint ourselves in.

Okay, it was no coincidence. I was an unabashed paint stalker. Once I saw Derek go for the blue tempera paint tubs, I did the same. Besides, painting myself in those hues would only echo the blue longing in my heart for him.

Oh, gag, that was over-the-top gross. When did I get so sappy? Why can't my brilliant wit and sparkling conversational skills ever come out too?

Why does Derek bring out this side in me?

He and I worked in silence for a good twenty minutes, painting in perfect harmony. I was aware of his hard thigh, an inch away from mine under the table. It was so tempting to shift just slightly in my seat, just enough to brush against his leg.

Geez, snap out of it! I was acting like a love-crazed freshman, not a mature, self-controlled professional cupid.

I forced my attention back to my self-portrait, scrutinizing what to do next. I'd already drawn the outline and was filling in the blue hues to add shading and depth.

"Your sense of proportion is really good," Derek said out of nowhere.

I looked up at him, blinking rapidly. "Who, me?"

He grinned crookedly, one eyebrow shooting up at me. "Yes, you."

"Oh. Okay."

I mentally smacked my forehead. That was smart. He'd given me a compliment . . . a weird one, but a compliment nonetheless. Maybe I could act like I had half a brain.

"I mean, thanks," I continued. "Yours is . . ." I looked closely at his painting, trying to find the right compliment to give him back. Everything looked fantastic—he'd even captured his own strong jawline and the wave of his hair perfectly.

"Your painting is just incredible, Derek. You're really talented." I finally said, daring a glance at his face.

"Thank you." His eyes locked with mine for a moment, and I felt a crazy, impulsive urge to spill my feelings. Would he freak out if I told him how badly I had it for him?

Was there any chance he could feel that way too?

Only one way to find out. I parted my lips to speak, willing myself to let whatever needed to be said just flow out of my mouth.

"Okay, the bell's going to ring any second," our art teacher said, his low voice cutting me off. "Pack up your paints and put your projects away, people."

Derek closed the light blue paint tub. "Thanks again for sharing your paint." He lifted his wet canvas and moved toward the art shelf, totally unaware of how close I'd come to confessing my undying love.

What was I thinking? Just because Derek had looked into my eyes so boldly, I'd suddenly wanted to tell him all those embarrassing feelings I had for him.

I had to be losing it. That was not one of my better ideas, and if it weren't for the art teacher, I'd have made a total fool out of myself.

I packed up my stuff and darted out the classroom door, weaving rapidly through the students in the hall to escape. I didn't know how much longer I could handle this, but something was going to have to give.

When I reached the comfort of my home, I darted upstairs and hopped on my computer, booting it up. I created a blog entry, locked just for Andy and Maya to read:

> *I almost did the dumbest thing today, guys. I was*
> *thiiiiiis close to spilling my guts to Derek. Honestly, I*
> *don't know why! There was just something about the*
> *way he was looking at me. Gee, I must love torture.*
> **sigh**

"Felicity, you here?" I heard my mom call from downstairs.

"Yup, I'm in my room."

"Can you come down and help with dinner? I'm making enchiladas tonight. You know how your dad loves Mexican."

I tried not to roll my eyes. Ever since I secretly matchmade my folks last month as an anniversary gift to help them renew their affection for each other, they've been super lovey-dovey. Okay, not nearly as bad as they were while under the two-week spell, but still. I could do without all the gooey attention they give each other.

"I'm coming," I said, posting my blog entry and closing my PC down. I could only imagine what comments the girls would leave when they read my post.

I shuffled downstairs, rolling up my sleeves. I probably should have put a bib on, given how messy I tended to get when cooking. Not my mom, though—she was always pristine and pulled together. Sometimes I wish I could be like her . . . until I start remembering what a control freak she is. Yeah, not my style.

Mom pointed toward the stove, where the frying pan was already perched, a pile of tortillas on the countertop beside it. "I need you to fry those up and dip them in the enchilada sauce," she said.

"Okey dokey."

We worked in silence for a few minutes—me frying like a diner cook and Mom preparing the filling.

"So, what's going on with school? Any guys tripping over themselves to date you?"

I scoffed. "Right. Because I'm such a beauty queen."

"Hey, don't sell yourself short," she chastised, pointing a finger at me. "I happen to think you're very pretty."

Well, that was nice of her. Mom wasn't one to dole out compliments a lot, so I knew she meant it.

"Thanks," I said, hoping my earnestness rang through in my voice. "I wish—" I stopped myself, not wanting to go into how badly I wanted Derek to feel the same way I did.

Mom, though, must have known what I was going to say. She nodded her head, shooting me an empathetic look as she filled the tortillas and wrapped them into cylinders, lining them up in neat rows in the baking pan.

"Guys don't always pick up on things when they should, especially when it comes to matters of the heart," she said. "You know, back in high school, it took a while for your dad to see me as more than a friend."

"Really?" Mom never talked to me about how she and Dad ended up together. And I never asked, not wanting to pry, but also trying to avoid the ick factor of thinking about my parents in that way. "I always figured you two were instantly in love." I popped the last tortilla into the frying pan.

This time she was the one who scoffed. "Hardly. For a long time your dad was oblivious to anything but football. I had a crush on him for a full year before we started dating."

"So, what changed, then?" Mom can be a little stuffy sometimes, but maybe back then she had a trick or two up her sleeve on how to get a guy's attention.

She stopped folding enchiladas, dropping her voice and leaning in to me. "Honestly, I don't know. One day he came up to me out of the blue and asked me on a date. We've been together since."

I chuckled. Someone must have hit him with Cupid's trusty arrow. "Funny how that works."

The front door opened. Mom wiped her hands clean on a dish towel, then winked at me. "Speak of the devil. That must be your dad." She headed out of the kitchen, and I heard her say, "Hey, honey. We're making enchiladas."

"Fantastic. Thanks!" he exclaimed.

Kissy sounds came from the living room. Oddly enough, I didn't feel as horrified as I normally would. I guess hearing that Mom went through the same kind of rough time I was in made me feel a little less squicked out. It also helped that they were fully clothed and not getting it on. Thank God.

I finished making the enchiladas, poured sauce over them and sprinkled on the cheese, as Mom had been doing, then popped them into the oven. I could be the good daughter and give them a minute to themselves. It wasn't like I was getting any romantic moments of my own anyway.

"This was such a great idea, Tyler, to have a group date!" Andy proclaimed later that evening. After a good half hour of loving gazes, she finally took a moment to peel her eyes away from Tyler to look at me, Maya, and Scott, all seated around a table in Starbucks and holding steaming coffee cups. "Thanks again for coming out with us, guys."

"You're welcome," Maya said with a smile, giving Andy a knowing look. "Like we'd say no to you." She took a sip of her drink, then snuggled into Scott's side. He lifted an arm and wrapped it around her.

I wiggled over a little bit to give them more room.

Andy and Tyler started whispering to each other again, their faces mere inches apart. I looked at the two of them with half amusement, half pride, knowing the love spell I'd cast on them earlier today had obviously done its job. They'd been inseparable all evening.

As soon as I'd finished eating dinner, a breathless Andy had called me, saying Tyler had asked her out on a date for tonight. But she'd already planned to chill with me and Maya at Starbucks and had regretfully let him know. Therefore, Tyler had suggested all of us get together as a group.

Of course Maya and I agreed—that's what friends do for each other. Besides, it was painfully obvious Andy was desperate to go out with Tyler, and it was a great opportunity for me to view the newly made couple.

So there we were, in Starbucks, where happy couples in love cuddled, sipping coffee and whispering sweet nothings in each other's ears.

Oh, wait, except for me—a.k.a. "the fifth wheel."

I had never felt so painfully out of place. My discomfort was highlighted by the lovey-dovey smiles passing every millisecond between the two couples.

Not that I wasn't thrilled for them, because I totally was—I'd matchmade them, after all, and I took a great sense of pride in the job I did. It's just that watching Scott and Tyler so enraptured with my friends made me realize I was never going to have that with Derek, no matter how much I tried to fool myself.

It was pathetic, really, to keep chasing after a guy who wasn't going to look at me that way. *I* was pathetic.

Let it go for right now, Felicity, I ordered myself. Right now was about Andy, not me. I needed to buck up and hide the little green monster lurking deep in the back of my brain. This was not the time to be jealous of my best friends. They couldn't control Derek or his feelings.

And actually, neither could I.

Maybe it was time to move on from my crush on Derek, once and for all. Because as long as I let myself think about him romantically, I knew I'd always be hoping there was a chance to make it work. Why keep torturing myself like that?

"What's wrong, Felicity?" Maya asked. "You have a big frown on your face."

I forced a smile. "Oh, nothing," I replied. "I . . . burned the roof of my mouth on my coffee. You know how badly that hurts."

Maya nodded in empathy. "I sure do. Scott and I went to a movie last week, and I actually burned my tongue on the nacho cheese in the theater. Nacho cheese—who knew it could even *get* that hot?"

Andy leaned over toward Tyler and whispered something in his ear. He sucked in a quick breath, nodded, then kissed her.

Yeah, it was time for me to go. These lovebirds needed their privacy, and I felt like a perv watching them.

I glanced at my watch. "I gotta run. I need to cram for my

English quiz tomorrow. You know Mrs. Kendel will crack the whip on me if I don't do well. And that's not half as bad as my folks would be." I slid out of the booth before anyone could protest. "Have fun, you guys!" I said in an overly bright voice.

"Bye!" Andy said. "I'll talk to you tomorrow, 'kay?"

I gave her and Maya a quick hug, waved to the boys, then took off from Starbucks, heading to my mom's car in the unseasonably warm late April air. I slid into the driver's seat and headed home, a plan formulating in my mind.

I needed to find Derek a girlfriend. If he was unavailable to date, I would be forced to move on. Maybe I could even find love somewhere else someday.

I almost laughed out loud. I knew that wasn't likely to happen, but I needed to do something drastic to get over him.

I pulled into the driveway, then exited the car and headed inside the house. I trudged to the kitchen.

"Thanks for letting me borrow the car," I said to my mom, dropping the car keys into her open hand. "I think I'm going to go study for a little bit."

She pinched my cheek with her other hand, smiling. "My little studious girl."

I rolled my eyes, laughing. "Oh yes, you know me. The total nerd."

"Well, don't forget to fold and put your laundry away," Mom said. "I left the basket on your bed."

I saluted her. "Sir, yes sir!"

She swatted me. "Get out of here, smart mouth."

Upstairs in my room, I popped in a CD, then grabbed my PDA and turned it on. Perched on the side of my bed, I stared hard at Derek's profile, the pixels taunting me.

Name: Derek Peterson

Age: 17

Interests: Excellent athlete in football. Highly gifted artist. Witty sense of humor, and very intelligent. In all honors classes. Drives a Chevy Cavalier. Is superfriendly to everyone.

Style: Casual jock

Okay, think this through. Who would be the perfect match for Derek?

I lay back on my bed, closed my eyes, and blindly grabbed for my pillow, plopping it over my face. I needed to shut out all distractions, including Justin Timberlake, who was currently crooning in the background.

I sat straight up in bed as a flash of inspiration hit me, the pillow falling onto my lap. What if I paired him with Britney? She was a nice, attractive girl I'd set up in my very first cupid match. That pairing didn't work out, because the guy had turned out to be totally wrong for her, but Britney had survived the heartbreak and grown more confident and outgoing since then.

It would be a good way for me to make reparations for pairing her with an utter bonehead the last time. And I knew Derek would treat her right, because that's the kind of guy he was. He'd be the best boyfriend a girl could have.

Surely she'd make Derek happy as well. He deserved to be with someone who would strive hard to keep their relationship working. Someone who would appreciate how amazing he is.

I swallowed down the lump in my throat. This would truly be the most generous gesture I'd ever made in my life.

I turned on the PDA and drafted the blank e-mail to Derek, then quickly flipped through the address book and carbon-copied Britney. Closing my eyes, I pressed send, ignoring the twisted feeling in my gut.

I was setting Derek up to be in love with someone else.

I opened my eyes and glanced back at the LoveLine 3000.

Maybe I could matchmake another couple to help take my mind off Derek. I did, after all, have a weekly quota to fill. *Who's been single for a while?* I sorted my profiles and came up with a name at the top of the list: James Powers.

Oh, geez. The comedian himself, with no girlfriend? What. A. Surprise.

With a big sigh, I flipped through the list of students until I found someone who might like James. Mitzi from health class would be perfect—she was a total ditz and always giggled at everything. Maybe she'd think his armpit farts were funny. And I just so happened to know that she and her boyfriend broke up a few weeks ago.

I sent them the love e-mail, then turned off my PDA. I'd had enough matchmaking for the day.

Chapter 3

The next morning when I got to school, it was deserted. Well, there were cars in the parking lot, but no people roaming around outside like usual. Maybe school was canceled, or maybe there wasn't supposed to be any school today. That would be a nice surprise.

I checked my PDA's calendar to make sure it wasn't a teacher's in-service day. Nope, all was normal.

Cautious, I stepped toward the double doors, waiting to see if something weird would happen. A sudden cheering sound to my right caught my attention, so I headed in that direction instead. The sound had come from the track field.

Wow. Hundreds of students—and teachers—packed the overcrowded bleachers, waving and hollering. Was there a morning track meet I didn't know about?

I pushed through the crowd and made it to the edge of the wire fence surrounding the track. There was only one person out there, running laps.

Derek.

"Oh my God," a student whispered behind me, "isn't he the hottest? Why didn't I ever notice it before?"

A guy beside her nodded enthusiastically. "Look how well he runs," he said, awe practically oozing out of his voice. "One foot in front of the other. No tripping. You'd think he invented the sport of running with those skills. No wonder he's so good at football. Think I can get his attention?"

"As if," a girl with a nose stud and purple hair said, her tone huffy. "Derek walked past me earlier this morning and said hello. It's obvious he's interested in *me*." She sighed deeply, unable to peel her eyes off him.

I spun around, my eyes raking the crowd. All these people were here to watch Derek run? What was going on here? Since when was our school so wrapped up in running?

"Dude," some guy said, "Derek is the best. Don't know why, but I just . . . feel the urge to be around him."

His buddy, a big burly guy, nodded in response. "Me too. Weird, huh?" He glanced around, his eyes taking in the group of students pressed against the fence, all watching Derek run laps. "Seems like everyone else here does too."

A sinking feeling plopped into the pit of my stomach. Something told me this was probably my fault.

I withdrew from the crowd and dashed into the school building. After looking around to make sure I was alone, I opened my LoveLine 3000. I looked at the sent messages. Okay, the love e-mail to James and Mitzi went fine. I scrolled down to Derek's e-mail.

And found that I'd accidentally CC'd the entire school.

Oh, crap.

"Hey, Felicity," Bobby Blowhard said from right behind me.

I crammed the LoveLine 3000 into my pocket and spun around, nearly smacking into him.

I bit back a sigh. "Hey," I mumbled in response. Bobby was the last person I'd wanted to see, and the tight, sleeveless top he was wearing was a vivid reminder of that.

I was trying to formulate an escape plan when a thought hit me. "Wait a minute—how come you're not outside with everyone else?"

He shrugged. "I don't know what the big fuss is. So Derek can run. Big deal."

It didn't make sense. If the whole school was now in love with Derek, why wasn't Bobby out there too?

"Don't you still have e-mail?"

"Sure, but my computer crashed a couple of days ago, and I can't get on there. Anyway, I'd rather talk face-to-face." He gave me a big, wolfish grin and leaned toward me. Like that was going to lure me to the dark side. "Why, did *you* want to talk?"

I bit my lower lip to keep from laughing. Oh, great. No wonder he wasn't all over Derek's ass. And of course it was my typical luck that *he* was the one person in school who hadn't checked his e-mail.

"I'd better go," I said, moving away from him toward my first-period English class. "Mrs. Kendel gets mad if we're late." I darted off, throwing a quick "bye" over my shoulder.

The rest of the day was just as odd. Classes went on as usual, but in between classes, Derek's name must have popped up in every conversation I heard, between both guys and girls, students and teachers:

"Derek's so handsome. I love the way he styles his hair."

"Derek said he and I are going to play some football tomorrow night."

"Guess what? Derek touched my arm today when he was reaching around me to grab a Coke. His hands are *so* warm."

And so on.

Not that I was eavesdropping. They just made it very easy for me to listen.

One good thing I noticed was that the other love matches I'd already made weren't affected by the Derek e-mail. Probably the rules about this were explained in my cupid user's manual, but that thing was waaaay too long and complicated for me to be expected to read. Maybe once a one-on-one love match was made, it would stick until the sparkles wore off, no matter what other arrows were shot—or e-mails sent, in my case.

That was a good thing in some ways, but had one drawback I hadn't predicted: If I wasn't listening to people moan forlornly about Derek, I had to listen to Andy rattle on and on about Tyler.

And talk, she did:

"Oh my God, Felicity, did you see the way Tyler answered Mr. Wiley's questions so fast? He's so smart—who knew he was soooo good at anthropology."

"Tyler looks so good in Abercombie and Fitch."

"I love the way Tyler holds his drumsticks."

"Tyler blah blah blah . . ."

Help. I'd created a monster!

My only consolation was that he seemed as equally in lurve as she did. In classes and at lunch he spent most of his time staring moony-eyed back at her.

Even art class didn't give me the thrill it normally did. We finished our monochromatic portrait early in the class period. Our art teacher, Mr. Bunch, then set up a still life for us to draw with charcoal . . . and proceeded to spend the entire hour giving Derek one-on-one instruction, praising his "profound" and "innovative" techniques with the charcoal stick.

Mr. Bunch started getting possessive of Derek's attention, which was kind of creepy. One guy in class complained because he didn't get a chance to hover over Derek and was immediately sent to detention.

Derek smiled and treated everyone fairly, but I could tell he wasn't nearly as in love with everyone as they were with him. Which made sense—his love was divided among the entire student body. Sans me and the couples I'd matchmade. And Bobby Blowhard, of course.

The last bell rang. With a heavy heart and a guilty conscience—

after all, I'd caused all this mess—I gathered up my materials, slung my backpack over my shoulder, and plodded my way to the library. Andy was *supposed* to study for our health quiz with me today, but during lunch she said she was going to listen to lover boy's band practice for some upcoming party, so I was on my own.

I found a thick wooden table in the very back and opened my book, turning to the chapter where I'd left off yesterday. I read the first few lines of the page about four times, but couldn't concentrate. I closed the book and dropped my head into my hands.

I'd made such a huge mess of things. Again. What if Janet fired me?

Or, even worse—what if she sued me?

I swallowed hard and slouched in my seat, glancing furtively around me at the empty room. Did anyone suspect I was to blame for the Derek lovefest? What if they sent me to jail for messing around with people's lives like that? If it isn't illegal to screw around with people's hearts in that way, it should be.

I'm way too soft to go to the joint. There's no way I'd make it.

Oh, crap. Another thought hit me. Janet was going to see that I butchered this job when she looked at my PDA at our weekly meeting. And something told me this wasn't a mistake I should try to hide. Maybe it would look better if I came to her and fessed up instead of waiting to get busted.

I plunked my elbows onto the table, then cupped my head in my hands. This had all started because I was trying to do a selfless act. Note to self: next time, just be selfish.

A shuffling sound got my attention. I lifted my head and saw the very object of my desire—and everyone else's—dart into the room. Derek.

My heart almost jumped into my throat.

When he saw me, he froze. I could see the panic written on his face.

"Oh, sorry," he said. "I, um, just needed a place to study. Alone."

I sighed, disappointment spinning in my stomach. He thought I was just another groupie. I gathered up my materials and stood. "Be my guest. You can have the room. I won't tell anyone you're here."

Derek tilted his head and looked at me oddly. "Really? Oh. Well, you can stay if you want to."

"Um, okay," I said with a cool nod, trying to squelch my nerves. I just needed to play it casual. After all, I was alone, with Derek, in the library. No one else was around.

And I couldn't even drool all over him.

With a sigh of relief, he plopped into the seat opposite me at the table. "Sorry," he said, digging through his faded blue backpack. "It's been a weird day for me, in case you didn't notice."

I laughed and sat back down, pulling out my book again. "So I saw. You got girls hanging all over you."

He shook his head. "Not just girls. Guys, too. And teachers." Derek leaned forward, his eyes sparkling as he gave me his trademark crooked smile.

"Must be your cologne, huh?"

"Maybe. Eau de Derek must be a popular scent today." He laughed again, then looked at the book I had. "Oh, I had health class last year. Mrs. Cahill's quite a character, isn't she?"

I rolled my eyes. "Yeah. Now, we're talking about cholesterol and what clogged arteries look like. This book has some of the grossest stuff I've ever seen. I swear, I'll never eat meat again."

"I said the same thing. Two weeks later I was back at McDonald's. Obviously didn't last too long."

Holy crap, what planet was I on? I mean, look at me. I was sitting in the library, having a normal conversation with the guy of my dreams. And he seemed to like talking to me, too!

Maybe I really did have a chance with him. Maybe he and I could—

"I'm so glad you're here," Derek said, interrupting my thoughts. "It's nice to have someone around who just wants to be a friend."

And instantly my heart deflated. I swallowed hard and tried to recover from the crushing blow of the "just friends" curse.

"Oh, absolutely," I said, nodding like an idiot. A bobbing-headed idiot.

I was no closer to dating him than Bobby Blowhard was to dating me.

Chapter 4

Janet shook her head and looked at my PDA. "You sure did a number on this one. I can't even see how you copied everyone in the school."

I blinked rapidly, embarrassed. I felt so guilty about my error that I'd driven over to Cupid's Hollow to see her as soon as I left the library, asking her for an emergency meeting. Thankfully, she'd been able to fit me in.

"I'm sorry," I whispered, trying to swallow down the lump in my throat. "I'm so stupid. Is it fixable?"

She glanced up at me. "You're not stupid, you made a mistake. Don't worry about it. The magic will wear off in a couple of weeks, just like it does with every other love match."

I exhaled, the tension easing from my shoulders and neck. "Oh, thank God. I was afraid I'd created something very perverted . . . and permanent."

Janet scoffed. "Permanent? Hardly. Ever heard of the sixties' lovefests? The famous Summer of Love? Well, that was partly my fault."

"Really?"

"Absolutely. You're not the only person to ever make a mistake, you know. I was toying around with ways to create love matches other than bows and arrows and decided it might be fun to try adding the magic to Kool-Aid . . . not realizing *everyone* would be sharing it. I got some unexpected results from that experiment."

I watched her smile, her eyes staring off into space. Obviously, she had some good memories. I couldn't imagine Janet as a carefree hippie, though. It was so far removed from her current personality, which leaned more toward uptight.

"Yeahhhhhh, those were the days." Janet shook her head. "Anyway, that was a long time ago, and we've gotten better at matchmaking since then."

"Well, I'm glad to hear I won't cause any permanent harm."

"You didn't, but try to be more careful next time." Uptight

boss-lady mode was back. She scrawled something on her ever-present notebook, then glanced back up at me. "So, what are you going to do to fix the problem?"

Good question. "Wellllll . . . ," I drawled, trying to think fast, "what if . . . what if I started matching all those people up with each other? Since Derek's love for them isn't equal to theirs, maybe I can distract them with a new romance?"

Janet rubbed her jaw. "Interesting idea. Actually, that just might work. Since it's not a direct one-for-one match, the magic is probably more vulnerable. It might be worth a shot to try that tactic. Let me know how that works out for you."

"Okay, I will!" I sat up in my seat, suddenly excited. Things weren't hopeless, after all. Thank God, I could still fix this!

I made a new mental goal—to make as many love matches as I could in the next two weeks. Yeah, I had, like, more than three hundred couples to make, but I could do it, right? Nothing was impossible, especially if Janet gave me the go-ahead.

"Just make sure all the new matches meet the minimum compatibility requirements so the magic will take. Willy-nilly pairings won't cut it here. Is there anything else?" Janet asked, glancing at the clock mounted on the wall.

"Um, no, that was it."

"Great." Janet stood and smoothed her skirt.

Guess that was my cue to leave. I thanked her for being so understanding and headed home, careful to drive five miles under the speed limit so my stupid cop brother couldn't decide to play head games with me. He had a tendency to pull me over whenever he wanted, just for laughs. It drove me absolutely nuts.

Once I got home I popped into my room, draped across my bed, and opened my PDA, ready to make some love matches. Considering the magnitude of the job I was facing, I'd need a system to ensure the best quality matches possible in the shortest period of time.

So, I'd match people in their own classes—freshmen with freshmen, sophomores with sophomores, and so on. That would make life so much simpler.

But first, I'd match up couples who I knew were interested in each other. Pairs I'd noticed flirting with each other sometimes, or checking each other out in the halls.

Unfortunately, that list was small. I matched up the dozen or so obvious couples within just a few minutes, then stared at my huge profile list. So many people to pair off!

I spent the next hour making couples as quickly as I could. I got through about forty before my hands started to cramp from working on the PDA. So I put it down and stretched my aching fingers, then picked up the phone.

I dialed Andy, ready to chat with my BFF and see how her love life was progressing. Also, I wanted to get her take on the library encounter with Derek.

"Hello?" she said.

"Andy, it's me."

"Hey, Felicity. Hold on a sec, 'kay?"

"Oh, okay."

The line clicked, and then Andy's voice came through. "Hey, honey, that's one of my friends. I'm going to get her off the line so we can keep talking, okay?"

My throat closed up, and I forced my voice to stay low and even. "Andy, it's still me. You didn't click to the other line right."

She gave an uncomfortable chuckle. "Oh. Sorry, I'm just right in the middle of a really good convo with Tyler. I'll give you a call later tonight, okay?"

"Yeah, sure," I mumbled, my face burning.

We hung up.

I couldn't ignore the twisting sensation in my gut. Ditched. For a dude.

Andy had just broken our unwritten rule . . . again. First she'd bailed on our health class study date, and now this.

I shrugged and swallowed down the uneasy feeling that I was losing one of my best friends. She never would have done this before.

Well, things were different now. And since I was the one who had matched her up, I had to deal with it.

Maybe Maya would have better perspective on the issue. I picked up the phone to call her, but promptly hung it back up again. I needed some face time, and I knew Maya wouldn't ditch me. She'd be shocked to hear how the phone conversation had gone, but she would know how to smooth things over and make me feel better.

I dashed down the stairs, threw my coat and shoes on, and booked it to Maya's house. The snow, piled along the sidewalks, was finally almost melted because of the bright sunshine, but everything was slushy and gross. Luckily, the jaunt to Maya's house was fast.

I knocked on her door, and it opened just a second later. Maya's mom, Mrs. Takahashi, nodded to me.

"Oh, hello, Felicity," she said, smiling politely. "Please come in. Maya is upstairs."

"Thank you," I said, careful to scrape the crud off the bottom of my shoes before taking them off in the foyer and placing them in a shoe cubby.

I heard a heavy series of thuds as Maya flew down the stairs.

"Oh, hey!" she cried out, her face splitting into a huge smile. She ran over and hugged me tightly.

Tears pricked the back of my eyes as I hugged her back. "Thanks for being so warm and welcoming. It's nice to know when I'm actually *wanted*," I said, unable to hide the edge of sorrow—and, to be honest, irritation—in my voice.

Maya pulled back, studying my eyes. The smile slid from her face, and she frowned. "Hey, what's wrong? Did something happen?"

I swiped a hand across my eyes. "Wanna go up to your room and talk?"

She nodded, leading me upstairs and into her bedroom. I saw her trumpet on her bed.

"Sorry if I interrupted your practice," I said as I sat in her computer chair. Maya's fastidious about her daily trumpet time. But then again, that's why she's so good.

"No problem," she said generously. "I can always pick it up again later. Now, what's going on?"

I sniffled, then explained the phone diss that had followed the study session ditch. Maya remained quiet as I talked on and on, expressing my frustration over Andy's attitude change now that she had a boyfriend.

Maya nibbled on her lower lip. "I can understand why you felt hurt by that," she finally said. "You know, though, Andy had been single for a long time. So maybe adjusting to a new boyfriend was a bigger transition for her than any of us had realized."

"I guess that's true," I acknowledged, spinning the computer chair back and forth as I chewed on her words.

Andy has always been überpicky about guys, so she doesn't date a lot—at least, not seriously. I couldn't remember the last time she'd had a real boyfriend. I guess I'd gotten used to her being around whenever I wanted to do something. Maybe that was a bit selfish of me.

"Give it a little time," Maya coaxed. "Things will level out with her, just like it did with me and Scott. I know she'll find balance. She remembers who her friends are, and she won't forget us—she'll probably call you later to apologize for brushing you off."

"You're a good person. Okay, I'll give it a little more time and be more patient." I stood and hugged her. "Now, go practice your nerdy music."

She rolled her eyes, tucking a strand of long, black hair behind her ear. "You're just jealous."

"You're probably right," I admitted. "You're so talented at everything."

We headed back downstairs, and I left her house, feeling a little better. Maya and Andy are opposites—Andy's fiery, spunky, and bold. Maya is calm, soothing, and steady. Her advice was like a balm to my raw nerves, and I tried to keep in mind what she'd said: Andy would level out eventually. I hoped she was right.

I shuffled through my front door, mentally gearing up to make more matches.

"Oh, good, you're back just in time," Mom said, spraying the coffee table and rapidly wiping it down. "I need you to run to the store and pick up a few things for dinner."

Great. Fixing all my messes would have to wait.

Chapter 5

Wednesday morning at school I slipped into my first period English class, taking my typical seat beside Maya. Contrary to what Maya had said, Andy never did call me back. But in the spirit of being the bigger person, as well as a responsible matchmaker-slash-friend, I decided to let it go.

I glanced around the classroom. Most of the students were buzzing about Derek and how attractive he looked today in his dark orange shirt. But in the back of the room I noticed a couple I'd paired yesterday sitting beside each other, holding hands, and whispering into each other's ears.

My matchmaking had worked! There was hope after all.

"Let's get class started," Mrs. Kendel finally said. She handed out the new novel we'd be discussing in class—*The Scarlet Letter*.

Several students groaned when they saw the title.

"That's enough of that," Mrs. Kendel barked, pointing a thick finger at all of us. "This novel is not only relevant to the time period in which it was written, it's relevant now. It shows a culture that shuns a scandalous woman for not confessing the identity of her child's father. And moreover, it shows a woman trying to not let society define who she is."

For the next half hour we talked about the setting of *The Scarlet Letter*. I had to keep my hands busy taking notes so I wouldn't be tempted to grab my PDA and make more matches. Mrs. Kendel wasn't someone who would let something like that go—she'd surely snatch the PDA out of my grasp and keep it in her desk drawer for the rest of the week.

The bell rang, and Maya and I gathered our stuff and left class. I noticed DeShawn, one of the first guys I'd matchmaded, slip out the door to greet his girlfriend, Marisa. He kissed her on the cheek, and with fingers wound tightly, the two of them made their way down the hallway, waving hi to Marisa's friends as they joined the couple in their walk.

I guess they'd decided to give DeShawn a fair chance, after

all. Well, that was good. When I'd first paired the couple, Marisa's friends tried their best to encourage her to break up with him. But holding true to her love, she stuck with him.

"I'm so glad they're still together," I said to Maya, nodding my head toward them.

"No kidding. DeShawn's so different since dating her," she said. "I think she's been a good influence on him."

"Absolutely. I think—" I stopped as the hallway started to buzz with abnormally loud activity.

Then I realized why. Derek was coming down the hall, surrounded by a massive group of students and teachers.

"And speaking of different, what's up with that?" Maya said. "I don't understand why everyone is all over Derek. Didn't you tell them he's your guy?" she asked, her tone teasing.

I snorted. "If only it worked that way." I shrugged casually, trying to say as little as possible to not give away the real reason Derek was the center of everyone's attention. "I guess he's just the flavor of the week. I'm sure things will chill soon enough."

And now that I knew how I could help remedy that, I was going to be a busy, busy girl, making those new matches—not just for the students, but for the teachers!

"So, what are you reading today?"

I glanced up from my novel, my heart racing. Since my matchmaking mistake—okay, *massive blunder*—Derek and I had been meeting at the library after school, just to hang out. Today was Thursday, our third meeting in a row.

Nothing was set in stone, as we hadn't officially declared we'd meet, but I'd shown up every afternoon this week just hoping our "date" would keep happening.

It did.

And it was the biggest thrill and most crushing disappointment of my life.

After all, Derek only saw me as a friend, like he had said. And technically, I should only want to be friends too. Though to be honest, I hadn't managed to move past my romantic feelings for him at all. Spending these afternoon sessions with him was only making me more smitten.

What could I do?

I ached to be close to him, so friendship was the best chance I had right now.

I shot him a smile. "It's *The Scarlet Letter*." I set the book down.

"I didn't think you'd be here. Don't you have about a billion people trying to date you right now?"

He laughed, sliding into the seat across from me and plopping his backpack onto the table. "I had almost fifty love notes crammed into my locker, asking me out for Friday night." He dug into the bag and pulled out a huge pile of folded pieces of paper.

Holy crap, he wasn't kidding.

"Well, I'm sure this will go away soon enough," I said. And if I did my job quickly enough, it would.

He opened the note on top, covered with red lipstick kisses. "'Derek,'" he read aloud, "'when Mr. Stephanides asked who had read last night's homework, and you raised your hand, I just knew I wanted to be around you. You're such a smart guy. Wanna go out tonight?'"

"Wow."

He sighed and looked up from the paper. "Yeah, no kidding. I can't date them all. I do like them, but there just aren't enough hours in the day."

I tried to smile, but my stomach flipped as I thought about my private blog. All those entries with Derek's name written over and over. Was I really any less pathetic than the people who wrote him these notes?

Well, at least I wasn't sending them directly to him. And that's because I was a class-A chicken.

"It's hard to keep coming up with good reasons to say no, though," he continued.

I shrugged. "Just figure out something else to do and tell them that, unfortunately, you're busy, but thanks. That way, you can be nice about it and tell the truth without making them feel bad."

His face brightened up. "You're right. That's a good idea. What are you doing tomorrow night?"

Every skin cell froze in anticipation. "W-who, me?"

"Wanna hang out? We could catch a movie or have dinner or something. It would be nice to chill with someone not psycho. You know, as friends."

As *friends*. I was beginning to hate the *F* word. Blech. But since I was desperate to be closer to him, I immediately answered, "Yeah, that would be fun."

Now that we'd talked it was time to get down to studying. After cramming the love notes back in his backpack, Derek grabbed his laptop and anatomy text. I glanced back at my novel, pretending I was reading and being studious. In reality I was watching Derek's hands as he typed his notes.

He had long, strong fingers. Clean, short nails. Lean, muscled forearms. I had a sudden flash of imagining those hands on the small of my back as I was pressed up against him, dancing slowly at prom. He'd slide his hand up my back, caressing my shoulder blade, to rest those strong fingers on my neck, leaning me closer . . .

I had to stop this. I fervently dug through my brain for a question to ask him. Anything to get my mind off Derek's hands.

"So," I said, clearing my throat, "do you have any brothers or hands?"

A startled look swept across his eyes. "Huh?"

A slow burn crawled up my face when I realized what I'd said. "Er, sisters, I mean. Sisters."

Derek smiled. "Two brothers and two sisters, actually. They're all younger than me, though, so I have to keep them out of trouble."

I stared at him in shock. "There are *five* of you? At least I only have one brother—he's crazy enough. Wow, how does your mom find time to do anything? And how do you get a moment of quiet in all that chaos?"

Derek laughed. "Yeah, there's no privacy in our house. Our family is Catholic, and my mom is apparently pretty fertile," he said with a mock grimace. "She and my dad just smile and say, 'the more the merrier.'"

I chuckled. "At least they have a good attitude about it."

Derek got a thoughtful look on his face. "I try to do what I can to help. That's why I have to work so hard at football. I need to get a scholarship so I can go to college next year. With that many kids, they can't afford to pay for me."

I nodded, feeling a sudden swell of pride that Derek was opening up to me about his home life. I was learning new stuff about him every day, and he was just as cool as I'd suspected. "My parents are super tight with money. My mom won't give me money for anything, which is why I had to get a job."

"Oh, really? What do you do?"

"Um, I work for a matchmaking company. Filing and paperwork and such."

He stared at me for a long minute. In fact, it was so long, I started to feel a bit weird. Maybe he thought it was odd for me to work there.

Or, even worse, maybe he suspected that the Derek lovefest somehow led back to me. Crap.

"That's interesting," he finally said. "Maybe you can find matches for everyone in school, then, so they stop hounding me."

I gave him an uneasy chuckle. He had no idea how close to the truth he was. "Yeah, I'll get right to work on that. So, do you work anywhere?" I asked, eager to divert attention away from my job.

"Well, I work part-time at my dad's sports store." He smiled. "We're pretty athletically oriented in my family."

"I'm terrible at sports, but I was the goalie on my elementary school soccer team."

"Oh, that's cool. Did you like it?"

"I got bored really easily," I said with a laugh. "Unfortunately, I was more interested in catching worms and butterflies than actually defending the goal." I shook my head, smiling. "Needless to say, I was asked to refrain from playing the next year."

"Aw, that's too bad," he said, trying to keep a straight face. "I'm sure you were cute to watch."

My lips got tingly excited from the compliment. "Well, my mom didn't think so. Like I said, she's pretty tight with spending dough, so you can imagine what a waste of money she thought it was."

Derek shrugged. "Sounds like most moms, actually. Mine's no different."

I rolled my eyes sympathetically.

We studied in silence for another half hour. Derek studied his work, and I studied him. The last few days, I'd gotten to know him a little better not only by asking questions, but by watching him.

When he was deep in thought, he rubbed a hand across his jaw. While taking notes, his forehead crinkled, and he got a little line between his eyebrows as he typed. He was so unbelievably cute.

I thought about what he'd just said. Four siblings total—that had to be hard on him. Forced to be responsible, to be accountable for what the others did. My esteem of him went up another notch, if that was even possible.

Compared with Derek's, my life was a picnic. All I had to worry about was myself. My pain-in-the-butt brother was out of the house and on his own, even though he did come over a lot. And my parents would at least help pay for part of my college.

I bit back a sigh. God, how I looked forward to whatever Derek and I were going to do on Friday. Even though it wasn't a real date, I had a feeling it was going to be an interesting evening.

Chapter 6

"I just don't get this book," Maya said to me later that night. With a groan, she closed *The Scarlet Letter,* rose from my bed, and started pacing the floor. "Why wouldn't Hester just tell on the guy who got her pregnant so she wouldn't be thrown in jail and viewed as a slut by her whole town? It was as much his fault as it was hers."

I squinted my eyes, flipping through my copy of the book. "It's kind of romantic, actually, that she's willing to face public scorn to keep their love a secret."

"I guess. I just wish he'd been there more for her, like she was for him. She did everything he wanted of her." She glanced away.

Maya wasn't normally this downhearted. Something had to be bothering her.

I put my book down. "What's wrong? Is there trouble with Scott?"

"Nothing's wrong." She sighed. "Actually, Scott gets better every day. He's the most thoughtful guy I've ever known." She shook her head, as if to dismiss her thoughts, and shot me a smile. "Anyway, let's start figuring out the symbolism in here so Mrs. Kendel will think we're utter geniuses."

I was tempted to push the issue and ask more questions, but decided to let it go. Maya would talk when she was ready, and if there was a problem with her relationship, I'd figure out a way to fix it.

Hopefully, she was telling the truth.

"Okay," I finally said. "Maybe we can get our discussion on this book over before Andy arrives." A glance at my watch confirmed what I'd feared. "Though she's already a half hour late."

"Maybe she had some stuff to do for her mom," Maya offered, sitting back on the bed. "You know she sends Andy on some wild errands, like to find crazy herbs or vegetables for whatever trend she's into now."

"Yeah, maybe." I pushed down the irritation that had been growing in me since Andy first ditched us for Tyler and I tried to focus on *The Scarlet Letter*. But only half my brain was there, while the other half was wondering, *Where in the world is she? Why hasn't she texted Maya or called?*

"Okay, here are the symbols I wrote down in my notes," Maya said, reading back over her paper. "We have the big scarlet *A* on her chest. Um, the *A* stands for adulterer, though Hester eventually grows to wear the symbol with a sense of pride and refuses to leave town. But what does Hester's daughter Pearl symbolize?"

I shrugged halfheartedly, not really caring about the drama of Puritan America.

"You know, you should just call her," Maya suggested.

"I don't see why I should keep having to reach out to her. She should have been here. On her own. *Without* me having to nag each and every time. And if she's standing us up, she should bother to call and let us know." I crossed my arms over my chest. "Besides, I wanted to talk to her about my date—er, nondate date—with Derek. I thought all of us could go out together."

"And we still can," Maya said. "If you just call her. She could have a very good reason for not being here."

"Maybe you're right." I wanted to believe Maya, wanted to feel like my friend wasn't ditching me yet again—and for a guy, at that.

I grabbed my phone from my bedside stand and called her. No answer.

"Hey, Andy," I said to her voice mail, trying to keep my voice light and nonreproachful, "It's Felicity. We were supposed to meet at my house for studying tonight. I wasn't sure if you forgot. Maya's here too. Anyway, give me a call." I glanced over at Maya, who nodded in encouragement for me to continue. "Um, I also have some news I wanted to talk to you about."

I hung up.

"Good." Maya smiled. "She'll call you back. In the meanwhile, let's get back to business."

"So what were we talking about?" I asked, trying to refocus. Maya was showing great patience with my griping, so I didn't want to keep blabbing on about Andy and end up irritating Maya in the process.

Maya and I studied for another hour, then called it a night. She went home to have dinner and finish the rest of her homework.

I checked my phone to make sure it wasn't broken or disconnected or muted or something.

Nope, working fine.

I went downstairs to heat up some dinner for myself. All that studying and fretting had made me hungry. Mom and Dad weren't home, having gone to Grandma's house earlier in the afternoon. But my mom had left me some lasagna in the fridge.

After wolfing down my food, I popped the dishes in the dishwasher, then trudged back upstairs to finish the rest of my homework and make some more love matches to help correct the Derek mess. What a lively evening I had planned for myself.

I cracked open my American History book and read the assigned chapter, taking notes as I went along. Mr. Schrupe had said he would be testing us tomorrow, and I had a bad habit of not paying attention in his class when he talked. I couldn't help it, though—the man was as dry as yesterday's toast. But I needed to pay attention to the chapter and do a good job so I wouldn't feel so guilty about my slackerly ways.

My phone rang, jarring me out of my reading. I grabbed it—the caller ID said Andy's number.

"Hello?" I said cautiously, wondering what excuse I was going to hear. If she said she was too busy playing tonsil hockey with Tyler to come study with me and Maya, I was going to throw up all over my phone.

"Heyyyy," she said, sighing heavily. "How did the study session go? I'm so sorry I couldn't make it. I had to fill in for one of the other servers at The Burger Butler. I just got home a few minutes ago. I'm exhausted."

My heart thudded in surprise. And guilt.

So she didn't ditch us for Tyler. Whoops. Maybe it would do me some good to stop jumping to conclusions so quickly.

"Oh, don't worry about it at all," I said, overenthusiasm pouring into my voice and making me blabber on and on. "We just discussed the book we're reading in English. *The Scarlet Letter.* Are you guys reading that one too? Anyway, sorry you had to work. I bet that sucked."

"Actually, we're reading *The Hobbit* right now. I think I like the movie better." She chuckled. "So, you said you had some news. What's going on?"

I briefly filled her in on Derek sort-of-not-really asking me out.

She squealed. "Really? That's so cool. I knew he'd come around to it one day."

"Thanks, but it's not like that. We're just friends."

"But after this date, that'll change. You know, Tyler says Derek is a really cool guy. And he's a good judge of character."

I didn't necessarily need the Tyler Seal of Approval, but I could be amenable.

"Well, speaking of," I said, "I was hoping you and Tyler would come with us. Maya already said she and Scott would come. Wouldn't that be fun?"

Not being a fifth wheel for once would be a miniblessing. And making it a group date instead of one-on-one would remove some of the pressure, and distract me from spending the entire time just wishing Derek saw me the way I saw him. I didn't think I could handle a whole evening of that.

"Definitely! I know Tyler will love that. Hold on a sec." She cupped her hand over the receiver and shouted, "Yes, Mom, I'm coming!" She uncapped the phone. "Sorry, gotta run. Mom's nagging me again. I swear, she can't do anything by herself. I wish she'd just hire a pool boy to entertain her for a while."

I laughed. "Maybe you could save up your extra money from working and buy one for her. Oh, and let me and Maya know when you do so we can come by. Um, for moral support, of course."

"Hah. You know it."

We hung up. I placed the phone back in its cradle, feeling worlds better. Andy, Maya, and I were going out on a triple date (okay, it's a date in the loosest sense of the word, but whatever). Once Derek and I had a chance to talk outside of school in a group date, where I could relax and be myself, he could see how charming and fun I am—not just how love struck and tongue-tied I tended to be around him.

With a jaunty hum, I whipped out my handy LoveLine 3000 and started making some matches. After all, since I was on the edge of something marvelous, it was time to pass that on to my fellow students.

Chapter 7

T minus twelve minutes until Derek showed up for our nondate date.

I sat on the couch in the living room, trying not to stare at the clock. My shaky fingers kept fidgeting with my freshly done hair. It was styled, but not too much so.

I wore my favorite jeans and a hot-pink T-shirt with cute little cherries on the front. An overall look of hotness without trying to look hot.

At least, that's the effect I was going for. Since it wasn't a real date, I didn't want to look like I was making more effort than necessary, or he'd be turned off. But I still needed to look hot enough to make him notice me in a nonfriendly way.

Being a girl was enough to drive me crazy sometimes.

Andy, beside me on the couch, patted me on the back. Tyler was going to meet us at my house too, and we would all ride in his car to dinner and a movie, where Maya and Scott would be waiting for us. After the movie the girls and I would crash at my house for our weekly TGIF sleepover, where we could blab all night about how the evening went.

"Chillax, Felicity. It'll be fine."

I nodded solemnly. "Does my outfit look okay?"

"Stand up."

I did so, slowly turning around.

Andy scrutinized my outfit with the utmost seriousness. She totally got how important this was to me. "Looks good to me," she finally said. "Hot, without looking like you put in too much effort trying to be hot."

I sighed in relief. "Oh, thank you! That's exactly the look I was going for."

The doorbell rang. Heart thudding painfully, I glanced at the clock—Derek was several minutes early. At least he wasn't going to keep me waiting.

Andy quickly squeezed my hand. "Keep your cool. You're sexy, and you own it."

"Thanks." I shook my head to clear the cobwebs, sucked in a deep breath, and pasted on a smile as I opened the door.

It was Tyler.

My shoulders slumped, but I fought to keep the smile on my face and the disappointment out of my voice. "Oh, hey, Tyler. Glad you made it. Andy's in there." I hitched my thumb behind me.

"Felicity, who's that?" my mom hollered from upstairs.

"Just Tyler. We're waiting on Derek, and then we'll be taking off."

"Well, be careful. Take my cell with you, just in case. I expect you home by ten."

I rolled my eyes and tried to smile at Andy and Tyler, who were now cuddled on the couch. "Sorry," I whispered, closing the door. "You know how moms are."

The door stopped right before closing. "Um, hello?" came a voice from outside.

It was *him*.

I tugged the door back open, cheeks flaming because I'd tried to close it in his face. "Oh, sorry, I didn't see you there."

Derek looked . . . well, he looked great. A soft, gray, long-sleeved T-shirt accentuated his muscled shoulders. He wore faded jeans with a pair of dark gray Skechers.

He looked at me, a small smile on his face. "So, can I come in?"

Duh. "Oh, yes, sorry. I spaced out there for a second." I held the door wider so he could pass.

Andy, Tyler, and Derek said their hellos. I hurriedly grabbed the cell phone from the kitchen table, then ran back to the living room and grabbed my purse. "We're taking off, Mom," I hollered. "Bye." I hoped we could get out of there before she—

"Hold on a second," she yelled back, coming down the stairs. "Let me say hi to your friends first."

Crap. Here it comes.

Mom headed into the living room, tucking a strand of loose hair behind her ear. "Hi," she said, sticking out her hand to Tyler, then Derek. "Where are you guys headed tonight, and who's driving?"

"This is my boyfriend, Tyler," Andy said, sidling up to Tyler and pressing her chest against his back. She wrapped her arms around him tightly, then gave him a small kiss on the back of his neck. "He's driving. We're just going out to dinner and a movie."

Mom eyeballed them. I could tell exactly what she was thinking. Should she say something about Andy, whom she's known for years, inappropriately close to *a boy*? Or should she let it go, since she wasn't Andy's mom?

Fortunately for me, she chose the latter.

"That sounds fun," she replied, then turned her hawk-eyed stare to Derek. "So, Derek, I expect you to be responsible tonight too."

Oh, dear God. Like he was going to try to jump my bones or touch my naughty bits. The boy didn't even know I was alive, other than as a buddy.

"Mom," I growled through my teeth, "we're just friends." *Unfortunately.* "We're just hanging out as a group, okay?"

Derek nodded, his face serious. "I promise I'll watch over her and make sure she gets in on time."

Mom smiled broadly. "Thanks. I'd appreciate it. Felicity here," she said, giving me a knowing look, "thinks she's too much of a big shot to be watched over by her mom."

Fabulous. I was like a freaking preschooler being nagged not to eat paste.

"Mo-o-ommmm," I groaned, "pleeeeease. We gotta go. Maya and Scott are waiting for us at the restaurant."

Derek, trying to keep a serious face, bit his lower lip.

Mom laughed and chucked me on the arm. "Oka-a-aaaaay. Go. Have fun. I'll see you back here at ten."

I practically ran out of the house, sucking in deep breaths to calm down. She really was a piece of work sometimes. I'm sure she meant well, but seriously. Not cool.

We piled into Tyler's Ford Focus and took off—Tyler and Andy in the front, Derek and me in the back. Since Derek had long legs, he had to sit behind Andy, who pulled her seat up closer to the dashboard to make room.

Derek's left hand absently traced patterns on the middle seat. I tried to keep my cool, my brain whirring to figure out a way to get closer to him. Maybe I could lean extra hard into a curve, and oops—I'd fall right on top of him.

Nah, too obvious.

"—supposed to be pretty good, actually," Andy said, her hand caressing the back of Tyler's neck. "Right, Felicity?"

"Huh? Uh, yeah," I said, having no idea what she was talking about.

She didn't seem to notice, or care. "I can't wait to try their food." She perked up and looked at Tyler. "Oh, honey—this is our first Friday date out! I should have gotten you a card for it . . . I'm sorry."

"Don't be sorry, babe," he replied, glancing over at her. He stroked a hand across the back of her head. "I didn't think about it, either. So *I'm* sorry too."

I shook my head and glanced at Derek, who jokingly rolled his eyes. We shared a small chuckle at the gagginess known as Andy and Tyler's TRU. ULTIMATE. LURVE.

Things weren't much different in the restaurant. Derek had chosen a new, casual burger place with great atmosphere to give us all a chance to talk. However, there wasn't too much talk happening among the whole group. Instead, Andy and Tyler sat across from each other, hands linked and eyes locked. They were murmuring back and forth to each other, totally excluding anyone else from the conversation.

Maya and Scott were at least a little more social. They kept dropping all these couple-y inside jokes, but they did make a point of drawing everyone else into conversation.

Meanwhile, Derek and I pored over the menu, trying not to feel like the fifth and sixth wheels.

"Um," I finally said to him, "I'm thinking of trying the El Rancho Burger. What about you?"

"That sounds good." Derek pondered the menu. "Actually, I was thinking about the Sacre Bleu Cheese Burger with Le Crunchy Frenchy Fries."

I giggled. "Well, if that doesn't do it for you, you could always try the Leaning Platter of Pizza. Actually, that sounds ginormous. If you got that, you'd have to change into your fat pants."

Maya jerked her head over, jaw dropped and eyes wide.

When I realized what I'd said, I flinched. Oh man, that totally came out wrong.

I tried to backpedal. "Um, not that you'd have any. 'Cause we all know you're totally not—"

Derek held up a hand, chuckling. "It's okay. I know what you meant."

The waiter arrived, and Andy and Tyler stopped gazing at each other long enough to pick out something to eat from the menu.

After he left, Andy grabbed my hand and tugged me and Maya out of our seats. "I have to pee," she said. "And Felicity and Maya have to pee too."

We laughed.

"Well, okay then," I said.

"Go ahead," Scott said, waving us off. "We know girls can't go to the bathroom by themselves."

The three of us headed straight for the sink to scrutinize our reflections.

"I swear, I must be chewing my lipstick off," Maya said,

grabbing dark pink gloss from her purse and gliding it across her lips. "I just put this on right before we got here."

Andy glanced around the stalls, then looked back at the mirror, widening her eyes as she reapplied her mascara. "You guys, I think I'm head over heels in love," she breathed. The mirror fogged in a small circle in front of her mouth.

I froze in place, jerking my eyes to look at her. "In love? Don't you mean 'in crush'?" I choked out. She'd just started dating him, like, two seconds ago . . . and that was because of *my* matchmaking. Yes, part of me was glad to see Andy so happy, but the rest of me was shocked by how fast things were progressing.

"He's perfect," Andy said with a soft sigh. "Simply perfect in every way."

"He *is* a sweetie," Maya said, popping her lipstick back in her purse and turning to lean her backside against the bathroom sink.

"Yeah," I hesitantly began, fixing a smudge on my lower lip, "he's a great guy. Even though he tends to do the 'seafood' thing a bit too much."

Now that I thought about it, I hoped he didn't show us his half-digested food tonight. That would be nasty.

Andy laughed, fluffing her hair. "Oh, I know. But it's cute. Anyway," she leaned in closer, "I think I'm ready to do it."

"Do what?" Maya asked.

"Go all the way with him." She widened her eyes again to apply mascara on the outer corners of her upper eyelashes.

I ripped my gaze from the mirror and stared at her in shock. "What?"

"Andy, that's a big step," Maya said, her brow furrowed. "You guys haven't been together a long time. It's only been a few days. Are you sure you're ready for that? Scott and I have been together for a month now, and we haven't even talked about that yet."

"Tyler's the guy of my dreams. It's never gonna get more perfect than this." Dropping her mascara in her purse, Andy stepped away from the mirror and headed to the door. "Come on, you two. Our dates are waiting."

Oh God, what have I done?

Chapter 8

I hardly knew what to do with myself the rest of dinner. I tried to keep my attention focused on whatever conversation was going around, but all I could think about was what Andy had said in the bathroom.

She was ready to give it up . . . to Tyler? After only one date? I mean, he was a nice guy and all, but having sex was no small thing.

I shuddered.

Derek glanced at me, concern written in his eyes. "You okay?"

"Yeah," I mumbled, "just a chill. I'm fine now, thanks."

We paid our bill and headed back to our cars, dashing across town in time to catch the movie. It was some kind of psychological thriller Andy wanted to see. We headed into the theater, grabbed our tickets, and got seats.

Derek sat on my left side, his elbow rubbing lightly against mine on the shared armrest. Even as my skin got tingly from the closeness, I tried to remain relaxed and cool. *This is not a real date,* I chanted to myself.

Scott left to grab drinks and popcorn for him and Maya, who were sitting on the very end of our row. Tyler and Andy were already cuddling in the middle seats.

I chuckled under my breath, remembering the last time the three of us girls were here. That was when Maya was juggling simultaneous movie dates with two of the three guys I'd matched her with. What a nightmare that had been—I'd had to run into the men's bathroom to distract the guys so they wouldn't talk to each other and discover they were both out with Maya at the same time.

I think I was still scarred from what I'd seen in that men's room.

With a low laugh, I leaned to my right and said to Andy and Maya, "This should be better than the *last* time we were here, right?"

Maya shook her head, squinting at me. "Very funny. I don't even want to think about that."

Andy looked blankly at us. "Huh?"

"Remember the last time we were here?" I said carefully, trying not to give too much detail, since there were boys present.

She stared at me for another couple of seconds, then nodded lightly. "Oh, right. I forgot all about that." She stood up. "I'm craving some popcorn. I'll be right back."

Tyler immediately hopped up. "Me too, babe. Let's go together."

Fingers intertwined, the two headed back down the aisle.

Yowch. Andy's disinterest stung. I leaned back into my seat and sighed deeply, watching them go.

"Hey," Derek said, "you okay? You seem like something's on your mind."

"Well," I said, "I'm just nervous that Andy's over her head with Tyler. They seem to be getting into this awfully fast." There. That was the truth, without giving too much away.

"I understand. They seem . . ."

"Attached at the lips?"

"Yeah." He laughed.

"I know it." I turned in the chair to face him. "See, we used to make fun of girls who clung to guys like that. And now—"

"And now, she's one of them."

I shrugged, suddenly feeling guilty for griping on my best friend.

Derek nodded, catching my eyes. "People do weird things when they think they're in love."

"Yeah, that's true."

"Give her time. She'll get over the 'love glow' and come to her senses."

Oh my God, he was right. Why didn't I think of that? Once the love spell wore off, she would be more aware of what was going on and could make a clear-headed decision. It had worked for Maya— she was obviously more levelheaded and not so absorbed in her relationship now.

I perked up, suddenly feeling better. "Hey, thanks. You know, you're pretty good at giving advice."

"You would be too, if you constantly had younger brothers and sisters hounding you. 'He stole my Barbie!'" Derek mimicked in a high-pitched voice. "'No, I didn't! But if I did, it's because she took my G.I. Joe!'" He rolled his eyes.

"I'm sure it's been a blast for you," I said with a chuckle.

He nodded in agreement.

We sat in comfortable silence for a few minutes watching the previews. Scott returned, taking his seat beside Maya. Andy and

Tyler made it back to the seats just before the movie started.

The film was weird, but it went fast. It was one of those thrillers that gets a ton of ad hype. My brother would love it. I can't say I was totally into it, but I don't think I was the target audience. Everyone else seemed to dig it, though.

We left the theater and got back to the cars. Andy and I gave Maya a quick hug, since Maya needed to run home and get her clothes before coming to my house for the TGIF sleepover. We got in Tyler's car and headed back home.

As we rode, I couldn't help but steal little glances at Derek. And a couple of times, I caught him looking at me, too. My heart fluttered with each catch of the eye, but I was too chicken to say anything to him.

It's a good thing it was dark, because I could feel my cheeks burning.

Before I knew it, Tyler was pulling back into my driveway to drop all of us off. It was just before ten o'clock—Derek sure kept his promise to my mom.

Trying to push down the disappointment in my gut at the end of our nondate date, I pasted on a big smile. "Well, guys, it's been a blast."

Tyler planted a huge kiss on Andy's lips. "See you later, babe."

Inwardly I cringed at his frequent use of the word "babe." I don't know why, but I hated that word with a passion. It sounded so . . . cheesy.

Derek smiled at me. "It's been fun."

We stared at each other. For a moment I got the impression that he wanted to say more. But he didn't.

Seconds ticked by in silence, except for the sounds of Andy and Tyler making out.

Okay, then. I guess it was time to go. I got out and closed the door.

"Bye!" I said as perkily as possible, then crossed in front of the car, opened the front passenger car door, and tugged Andy out.

Andy and I stood in the driveway and watched both guys take off in their respective cars. Then we headed into my house.

Once I closed the front door, I flung my purse and body onto the couch, desperate to start analyzing the entire evening with Andy, and then rehashing it again when Maya arrived so I could get her perspective too. We needed to run through every conversation with a fine-tooth comb to see if I'd missed anything important . . . or if I'd done something stupid without realizing it.

"Oh man, that was too interesting," I started. "I don't know what to—"

Andy jumped a little, then dug into her pocket and pulled out her phone. "Oh, hold on a sec. My cell's on vibrate." She flipped it open. "Hello?"

Okayyyy.

I headed into the kitchen and grabbed the requisite rocky road ice cream and three spoons in anticipation of Maya's pending arrival. A staple of our post-guy encounters.

Andy followed me. "Oh, hey, sweetie," she said in a quiet voice into the cell. Probably trying to not disturb my folks, sleeping upstairs. "Aw, I miss you too."

Good grief. They just saw each other, like, two minutes ago.

"Is that Tyler?" I asked in disbelief.

She shushed me.

"Sorry, baby," she said into the phone. "What was that?" Pause. "Okay, sounds good. I'll see you tomorrow. Good night." She made kissing sounds into the phone.

I grabbed three bowls and started scooping ice cream into two of them, then glanced up at her. She still had the cell open and up to her ear.

"Hey, you didn't hang up," Andy said. She giggled. "Okay, let's hang up together. Ready? One . . . two . . . three." Pause. "Well, you didn't hang up, either!"

Oh, for God's sake.

I grabbed the phone from her hand. "Hey, Tyler. She misses you, but she'll see you tomorrow, okay? Bye." I closed it.

Andy snatched the cell out of my hand, fire blazing in her eyes. "How dare you! That was unbelievably rude."

"Oh, come on," I huffed, the irritation and frustration I'd been burying down in my gut over the last few days boiling right to the surface. "You two are getting downright disgusting with the lovey-dovey crap. 'I love you,'" I mock crooned. "'I love you more.' 'No, I love *you* more.' Blah, blah, blah." I pointed at her. "You're not acting like yourself."

And even more importantly, why was Andy doing this when she was *supposed* to be spending quality time with her BFF?

Andy stared at me in disbelief, her jaw dropped open. She crammed her cell into her pocket. "I don't wanna stay here tonight. I gotta go. Later." Andy grabbed her overnight bag from the living room and stormed out of my house.

I stared in shock at her retreating form. I couldn't believe she'd backed out of our TGIF sleepover. I mean, it was our tradition. A hallmark of our friendship.

She had to be furious with me.

Well, you know what? She was acting stupid. Just because she was in love—and not even *real* love, thank you very much—she had to go act all psycho now. Who wanted to be around that? She'd become the kind of person we always mocked.

Even my crazy crush on Derek never deteriorated into what she was doing now. Ditching your girlfriends for a guy is the ultimate betrayal.

I ate my ice cream and Andy's, stomped into the living room, and waited for Maya, willing myself to push the argument out of my mind. No way was this fight with Andy going to keep me down tonight. I was still going to have a good time with my *real* friend.

But I knew there was no way I was going to be able to let this go.

"Felicity, pay attention," Mrs. Cahill, my health teacher, said on Monday, her tone snippy.

A couple of people snickered.

My head jerked up from the doodle in my notebook. Mornings stunk, and this one was no different.

"Sorry. I'm trying," I grumbled.

Someone notably *not* here today was Andy, who usually sat on the other side of me. I wondered if she was absent because of our fight.

Mrs. Cahill flitted to the corner of the chalkboard. "Instead of making you take a final exam this year, I'm going to try something different."

Cheers filled the room.

"I figured you'd like that," she said, laughing. She turned and wrote on the chalkboard, SPECIAL CREATIVE PROJECT.

The cheers quickly died into groans.

She threw us a look. "Basically, you're going to pair up with someone else in the class and do a creative project about something we've discussed. It can be a videotape about how pregnancy, or bulimia, or drugs can affect a teen's life. It can be a story about eating the right foods. The more creative, the better. Have fun with it!"

This was going to be so. Awful. We had a couple of weeks to come up with some stupid project about health, of all topics. Yeah, tons o' fun.

Mrs. Cahill grabbed a piece of paper off her desk. "I've already paired you up with your partners, so no griping."

As she read down the list, a sense of panic welled in me. *Please don't let me be with someone lame.* Maybe praying would help. There was nothing worse than being stuck with a dud for a class project.

God, I promise I'll be a good girl, and I'll stop judging my brother for the tramps he dates, and—

"Felicity Walker and Bobby Loward."

I heard Bobby say, "Yessssss," in a soft tone under his breath.

Yup, it was official. My life was over.

Chapter 9

"So," Bobby said after class ended, hot on my heels, "when should we get together for our project? I already have some ideas...."

I dodged left out of the classroom, trying to shake him. "I'll have to let you know," I mumbled over my shoulder.

I couldn't believe my bad luck. But really, why was I surprised? After all, it seemed lately like everything I touched turned to crap. The reverse Midas touch.

"Okay, sounds good," he said.

I stopped suddenly, remembering I needed to swing by my locker since I didn't have my lunch with me. Bobby thudded right into my back, causing my books to fly across the freshly waxed tile floor.

Peals of laughter echoed through the hallway.

"Geez, Bobby!" I hunched over, scrambling to grab my stuff.

He helped gather the rest. "Sorry," he muttered, a dark blush working its way across his cheeks. "I didn't mean to run into you."

I sighed deeply, taking the papers out of his hand. It wasn't his fault I was fighting with Andy, and I shouldn't be taking it out on him.

"It's okay. Thanks for helping." I ripped a corner off my notes and scribbled my home phone number down. "You can call me here later tonight. We'll figure out what we're going to do."

Bobby shot me a huge smile. "Sounds good." He spun around and took off, then quickly turned around to wave. "Bye!"

I headed to my locker, scouring the hallways for any sign of Andy. This was probably the worst fight we'd ever had in the history of our friendship. She hadn't called me all weekend—something we've never done before. Going that long without talking was starting to make me feel a bit unnerved.

This was bad.

While I knew I was right in being so pissed off at her annoying behavior, a part of me felt guilty. Maybe I should have talked rationally to her instead of alienating her. Well, the love spell would be wearing off soon enough in any case—only one more week to go—so maybe I'd be better off playing it by ear. After Andy snapped out of her funk, she'd more than likely want to talk.

I loaded my books into the locker and grabbed my lunch bag, my head swirling with all these thoughts.

I hadn't heard from Derek all weekend either (not that I'd truly expected to), and I wondered what he thought about our Friday non-date date. Did he decide I was too lame to hang out with anymore? Was he going to meet me at the library today after school?

Only one more week until the spell wore off the entire student body. Would Derek still want to hang out with me after that?

Maya, who was sitting alone in the cafeteria, was already chomping into her sandwich.

"Hey," I mumbled, plopping into the seat beside her. I opened my bag and took out my stuff, but my stomach was twisted into a pretzel. There was no way I was going to be able to hold anything down.

She glanced up. "Oh, hey. I take it you didn't hear from her?"

I shook my head, the backs of my eyes burning. No way was I going to cry over this. With an angry swipe, I rubbed my hand over my eyes.

"Sorry. I didn't, either. Maybe she's sick or something," she offered, her eyes sad. I could tell she didn't believe it, though.

"Yeah, maybe she's sick. Or working late. Or maybe she forgot. She always has an excuse for everything," I pointed out.

Maya sighed, then took a sip of her Coke. "This sucks. I hate when everyone fights. I just can't get away from it."

"Who's fighting?" Scott asked, coming up from behind us. He moved into the other available seat beside Maya, placed his lunch tray on the table, then leaned over and kissed her on the cheek.

I stood and gathered my stuff, suddenly not feeling like being social.

"Oh, no one. It's no biggie," I said. "You two have a good lunch, okay? I'm gonna head to anthropology class a little early and ask the teacher a question."

It was a total lie, of course, but they didn't seem to notice.

"Okay, talk to you later!" Maya said. She slipped her hand into Scott's, and I left them in happy-couple bliss.

I sludged throughout the rest of my day until art class. Most of the students were still all over Derek, but the buzz about him seemed to have hit a plateau, which was good. And the students

I'd paired up with each other this past weekend were ignoring Derek completely.

However, as usual by now, my art table was almost deserted as at least half the class crowded around Derek's table.

I glanced at him from across the room. When I caught his eye, he gave me a heart-stopping smile and a small wink.

So he didn't think I was a total loser at all. My shoulders relaxed. I attempted to focus my attention on the floral arrangement we had to sketch.

"Pssst." Kristy, a bleach-blond girl who usually spent most of the class time socializing, wiggled her fingers at Derek as a cutesy kind of hello.

He glanced up and gave her a polite smile, then tucked his head back down to focus on his drawing.

She giggled and picked up her chair, squeezing it beside him.

Mr. Bunch glared at her. "Kristy, what are you doing?"

"I needed a better perspective," she said, blinking her eyes rapidly in a pseudoinnocent look.

"Don't bother Derek—he's concentrating on his art," Mr. Bunch grumbled, but went back to his grading book.

"Derek," Kristy whispered, "I have a question for you."

"Yes?"

My ears perked. I tried to pretend I wasn't eavesdropping by faking a deep fascination with my art project, but I was so being nosy.

"I was wondering, who are you going to prom with?"

I swallowed hard and jerked my head up, my hand suddenly shaking. I put my pencil down, afraid I was going to drop it.

"'Cause if you don't have a date, I thought we could go together," she finished, beaming at him.

His face pinched up. "Well, actually . . ." He stalled off, his eyes glancing around the room, looking desperate for help.

"He's going with me," I blurted out.

His jaw dropped, as did mine. I closed my eyes and licked my lips, struggling with what to say next. "I mean, well, he's going—"

"Yup," Derek said. "I'm going with Felicity. Sorry."

Kristy pouted again, this time at Derek. "Oh. I see."

For the rest of the period she sulked in her seat as several students in the classroom griped about Derek's prom date. With me. I've never had so many people glare in my direction before.

I don't think I actually breathed the entire time. Once the bell rang I darted out of the classroom and went straight to the library, anxious to talk to Derek in private so I could apologize.

Long minutes passed before he finally made it. I sagged in relief. Even if he was mad at me for my blurting faux pas, I could at least get this chance to make things right. I'd put him in a situation where he had to agree with my wild, hare-brained idea so I wouldn't be publicly embarrassed.

"Look, about what I said in there—"

"About the prom thing—" he started, then stopped when he realized we were talking at the same time.

I chuckled nervously. "Go ahead."

If I let him speak first, maybe I could try to save face, based on whatever he said. I could even say I was buying him some time to figure out who he really wanted to ask. Yeah, that would work. I'd look like I was being helpful, instead of desperate.

"Well," Derek started again, "I'm glad you volunteered to be my date, because I was going to ask you anyway."

I stared at him. Was I hearing him right? "Eh?"

He grinned. "I was going to ask you if you wanted to go with me. I had a blast hanging out with you on Friday, and I figured a no-pressure prom would be a lot of fun. What do you say?"

This was, like, the best and worst day of my life.

What could I say but yes?

"Of course I'll go with you," I answered, hoping the big faketastic smile on my face looked enthusiastic enough, but not *too* enthusiastic. Just-friends enthusiastic. "It'll be a lot of fun."

"Great!" Derek unloaded his anatomy textbook and notebook from his backpack. "Let's start studying."

I chuckled weakly, cracking open my anthropology book. "Oh, absolutely."

Liar. Like I was going to be able to concentrate on anything but wondering how I was going to fake my way through prom as Derek's friend.

At my Monday night work meeting, I filled Janet in on the status of my love matches. Of course, I conveniently left out the part about how half the school was still in love with Derek, and that the others I'd paired so far were matched up in desperation and would probably regret their kisses in a week's time. And, just as fun, that the match for Andy was going so well that I'd now lost my best friend—who, by the way, was about to give up the V for a guy she barely knew and was basically drugged into thinking she was head over heels for.

All in all, an eventful week, none of which I admitted to.

After she synched my PDA and paid me for the week, I went

home and returned Bobby's call. Actually, *four* calls. Mom had written the messages on a purple Post-it note.

Bobby and I came up with a tentative date a few days from now to plan out our health project. That settled, he tried asking me if I wanted to play some poker afterward, but I managed to avoid setting a date for that and got off the phone as quickly as I could.

Then, I popped over to my PC and logged on to my blog, setting it to diary entry so Andy and Maya could not read it.

> *This has been such a weird day. Andy still isn't talking*
> *to me. I don't think it's fair that she's turned into a*
> *total flake and has totally abandoned herself to love, but*
> *she's mad at me for staying true to how I am.*

I chewed one of my fingernails, my stomach twitching a little. That was a bit harsh.

> *Okay, maybe it's not fair for me to blame her this much.*
> *I just hope things will get better when the spell wears*
> *off. I've made such a mess of this, but at least the*
> *matches I made are going strong.*

Oh, and the most important news: Derek asked me to prom!

Yeah, it was only as a "friend" thing, but still . . .

I posted the entry, closed the browser, and shut off the monitor, a sudden wave of depression hitting me. The best thing in the world had happened to me, and I couldn't share it with one of my best friends.

I picked up my phone and dialed Maya.

"Howdy," she said upon answering. "I was gonna call you later tonight when I finished all my homework. Did you read the assigned chapter in *The Scarlet Letter* yet?"

"Actually, I have way more important things to discuss," I said, pausing dramatically. "Something big happened to me today."

"Ooooh, what? Do tell. I'm intrigued."

"I. Have a date. For prom."

"Shut up!" She gasped. "Who are you going with?"

"Derek," I breathed.

"Omigod, are you two dating now? When did this happen? I guess Friday's date made a bigger impression than we realized, huh?"

I shifted the phone to rest between my ear and shoulder. "Well, unfortunately, we're going as 'friends.' He's looking forward to a no-pressure event."

"But after you have the perfect prom date with him, the day where he sees you as the girl of his dreams, you'll be dating him for sure. I just know it."

"You think so?"

"I *know* so."

Maya always knew what to say to make someone feel better. "Thank you. It means a lot to me that you believe in me. Especially with . . . well, you know what's going on."

She sighed. "Yeah, I know. I hope everything will straighten out soon. I'd love for all three of us to go to prom together as a group. Wouldn't that be awesome?"

"That's what I want too."

We said our good-byes, and I hung up. I slouched my way downstairs into the kitchen, where my mom was drying the dinner dishes. "Hey, Mom."

She glanced at me over her shoulder. "Oh, hi. What's up? How did your work meeting go tonight?"

"It was fine." I paused, trying to lend importance to my next words. "By the way, I've got a date for prom."

"Oh, are you going with Derek?"

How did she know? She never failed to surprise me.

"Actually, yes. I thought you'd be more . . . surprised."

"Why should I be?" She hung the dish towel up to dry. "He's a nice boy. You're a nice girl. I'm not surprised he likes you."

"It's not even like that, though. We're going as friends. We're just buds, you know." For some reason I had the impulse to wipe away her know-it-all tone.

She raised one eyebrow at me. "Hmm. If you say so."

I sighed. "I'm going to take a shower. I need to hit the hay."

"Sounds good." Out of nowhere, she kissed me on the cheek, a gesture she hasn't done in years, and tucked a strand of hair behind my ear. "We'll talk tomorrow about your prom dress."

My prom dress! I hadn't even thought of that. As I headed back up the stairs, I bit back a squeal and did a little boogie.

Chapter 10

On Tuesday I came out of my trig class, starving for lunch. It was pizza day—luckily, not quadrangle school pizza, but real pepperoni pizza. Papa John's. I was practically drooling thinking about it.

When I got into the cafeteria, I grabbed a couple of slices and glanced around. Andy was sitting in the back corner with Tyler. They were whispering in each other's ears, and she had a huge smile across her face. Tyler grabbed the pair of drumsticks from behind him and started pounding out a rhythm on the lunch table.

My stomach clenched up. What should I do? Maya wasn't here to dole out any advice, since she had some kind of band practice she had to attend. Should I go over and speak to Andy, or wait for her BFF radar to pick up on my existence and signal me to come over?

Andy looked up, and our eyes connected. Her face looked sad at first. Then fire blazed in her gaze. She turned away from me and looked back at Tyler, pasting an overly fake smile on her face.

My mind quickly flashed back to Friday's bathroom conversation, and I worried if she and Tyler had had sex yet. I couldn't tell just by looking at her.

Tyler crammed a piece of pizza in his mouth and did the seafood stunt, and Andy laughed.

"Oh, Tyler!" she exclaimed loudly, swatting him on the arm. "You're such a goof!"

Fine. She wanted to be like that? Then I didn't care.

I parked it at a nearby table by myself, scarfing my pizza down fast. I didn't want to sit in there any longer than I had to.

Once I finished my food, I bolted to my locker. In the classroom to my right, I heard some hushed voices arguing.

"—don't think that's a good idea," a male voice said. "I have a game that Saturday. Plus, my parents would probably say no."

"Come on," a girl replied. "It's just one weekend. Can't you tell your parents you're staying with our family? And maybe miss just one game? For me?"

"But I haven't missed a game yet," he hedged.

Of course, by now I was dying of curiosity. With as much casualness as I could muster, I peeked into the room.

It was Jon and Megan, two seniors I'd matchmade a couple of weeks ago. I'd met Megan when I did a round of volunteering in the front office last year—she and I spent the whole time filing paperwork and giggling about the missed-day excuses people brought in.

I hadn't seen the two of them around since I sent the love e-mails. Maybe I should have been spending more time scoping their relationship out, though—by the sound of it, things weren't going well. I made a mental note to watch my other couples as well.

Megan leaned her back against the chalkboard, arms crossed as she stared at Jon.

He sighed heavily, rubbing a hand over his hair. "I have to think about it."

"Come on," she said, sidling up to him. "It'll be fun. My folks will leave us alone for practically the whole weekend."

Jon huffed, pushing away from the chalkboard. "I can't deal with this right now." He walked toward the door.

I jerked back toward the lockers, trying to make it look like I was searching for a friend in the hallway. Jon didn't even notice me as he stomped past.

After he left, I heard sniffling in the classroom. Megan was obviously distraught. Should I try to talk to her?

Tentatively, I tiptoed in.

Megan jerked her head over to look at me, then glanced away, wiping the tears off her cheeks.

"Sorry if I'm being nosy," I said to her, "but I heard you crying. Just wanted to make sure you were okay."

"Oh, hey, Felicity. I'm fine." Megan paused. "Except that he's such a jerk sometimes!" she blurted out.

"What's going on?"

"I tried to set up a weekend for us to get some alone time, but Jon doesn't want to go. He'd rather play golf than go with me on a getaway. I think he's just not into me anymore." She swallowed hard, then looked up at me with tear-rimmed eyes. "I don't know what to do! I'm trying to do something nice with him, but he won't see my side of things."

I wracked my brain for advice. "Maybe . . . you two just need a third party to help translate things."

"You mean, like a counselor?"

"Yes, exactly!" I latched on to the idea, which was growing bigger in my mind by the second. "Guys talk a different language than girls. You two just need someone to help you understand each other. Actually, I could even do it if you want." I lowered my voice. "I've helped a few of my friends out with love problems."

She sniffled. "That might work. But what if Jon doesn't go along with it?"

"I'm sure he will, if you ask him nicely."

After a moment Megan nodded resolutely. "Okay, I'll do it." She gave me a watery smile. "Thanks, Felicity."

"Great! Just call or e-mail me when you two are ready to talk."

We left the classroom, both of us in higher spirits than before. I drifted through the rest of my day, pleased as punch about how I helped Megan and Jon. Doing for others even helped me get my mind off my own personal drama with Andy. What dedication I had to this job, and to love! To helping my fellow teens!

Maybe they'd name a humanitarian award after me. The Felicity Walker Award for Caring Teens. Yeah, I liked the sound of that.

In the library I made a quick list of resources. After all, if I was going to give love advice, I should at least catch up on the latest trends.

1. TiVo the following shows: *Maury, Dr. Phil, Oprah,*
   and *Judge Judy*.

Yeah, I know *Judge Judy* isn't a counseling show, but she keeps a tight rein on her courtroom. I could learn a thing or two from her.

2. Check out some books from the library on dating
   and communication.

3. Ask a guy for advice on a guy's perspective of life?

Speaking of guys . . . Derek popped up in the library.

I gave him my biggest, most charming smile. "Well, you're here just in time. I need some help."

His eyebrow rose. "Oh, really? With what?"

"I need a crash course on how to think like a guy, and you're just the one to do it."

Derek smirked. "Oh, is that right? You need my help?"

"Yup. I'm trying to help a young couple in love save their relationship."

"How very selfless of you." His eyes sparkled as he shook his head at me.

"Yeah, it's my way of giving a little back." I laughed, trying to calm the flutter in my stomach. He was just so. Freaking. Hot. "Seriously, though, it's not that huge a deal. They're just having problems under-standing each other. I can help him understand girls, but it's the whole 'guy' thing I'm not fully up on." I gave him a meaningful look. "Yet."

Derek leaned back in his seat. "So, what do you need to know?"

"Oh God, where to begin? There are so many things confusing about your gender," I said. "For starters, what's with guys' fascination with boobs?"

His jaw dropped.

My stomach clenched in response when I realized what I'd blurted out. Oh. My. God. *What is wrong with me?*

"Bad place to start, huh?" A flush rose over my cheeks.

"Just . . . surprising," he said, blinking. "I wasn't expecting that."

I shrugged as casually as I could muster, trying to brush off my embarrassment. Bravely trying to rescue the conversation, I continued on. "Okay, scratch that question," I said. "Here's a new one. Why do guys get obsessive about certain things, then mad if a girl isn't on the same level as him?"

"Like what?"

I studied him, trying to figure out a good example without giving away too much of the situation between Jon and Megan. My eyes caught hold of his football jersey.

"Let's say . . . a guy loves football with all his heart," I started. "He watches every game of his favorite team, signs up to play fantasy football, even sleeps with the ball—"

Derek rolled his eyes, holding his hands up for me to stop. "Okay, I get your point."

I laughed. "Anyway, why does he get ticked off if the girl doesn't care about it as much as he does?"

Derek thought for a moment. "Well, some guys find their identities through activities. It makes us who we are, so if a girl doesn't 'get' these activities, we think she doesn't 'get' us." He shrugged. "I like football, but not to the point of obsession. Now boobs, on the other hand . . ." He leaned forward, then waggled his eyebrows exaggeratedly.

I reached across the table and smacked his arm, then crossed my arms over my chest and swallowed hard. I was suddenly very aware of my own rather small girl parts.

"Ha, ha. Very funny."

"Come on," he said, "I'm just teasing. You brought it up. I only said that to make you laugh." His mouth curled into a very sexy smile.

I stared at his lower lip. What I'd give to kiss him, just once. A real, honest-to-God kiss, where he didn't want to be "just friends" with me.

Maybe it could happen at prom.

Right. And maybe I'd suddenly grow a C-cup overnight.

"So," I said, desperate to get my mind off my small chest, "what else do you think I should know about guys?"

"Well, let me see." Derek scratched his chin. "We do care about how we look, regardless of what we say."

"Mm-hmm."

He looked me straight in the eyes. "And we're often too shy to tell a girl what we're feeling."

My heart jumped to my throat. "Oh?" I croaked out. Was he trying to tell me something? *Pleasepleasepleaseplease?*

He nodded. "And sometimes—"

"Oh, Derek!" a loud voice said with a giggle. "What a surprise. I didn't know you were here."

He whipped around, and I groaned at the sight of Mallory, my nemesis. Great. Way to ruin a magic moment.

She sidled up to the table and thunked down in the seat beside him. "This is *such* a coincidence. I just came here to study. Imagine meeting you here."

He smiled. "Yeah, I come here to study too."

Was that smile for real? He looked real. Could Derek possibly like *Mallory*?

I squinted, studying her too-shocked face. Wait, she *knew* he was here, the liar! She must have been following him. I felt like our own private sanctuary was now violated. Was no place sacred anymore?

"Mallory," I said, suddenly feeling quite catty, "it *is* quite a shock. I didn't know you even knew where the library was."

She shot me a sugary smile. "I can see why you'd think that. But *I* usually do well enough in my classes that I don't need to come here."

Ouch. Touché.

I gathered up my stuff. I'd had enough of her face and attitude to last me for a lifetime. "I'll see you later, Derek."

"Oh, okay. Bye!" He gave me a big grin.

I walked away from him, back straight and head held high, like I didn't have a care in the world. Yeah, who was the liar now?

Chapter 11

Later that night I held a large, neon blue satin monstrosity against my figure and stared at my reflection in the store mirror, groaning.

"It has a butt bow. For God's sakes, Mom, a butt bow!"

Was she really so clueless that she didn't realize the heinousness of this dress?

Mom laughed. "Fine. Go put it back and find something else. But no high leg slits or too much cleavage showing."

I caught her eye in the mirror. "Right. As if I need to worry about that."

I returned the dress to the rack, wishing I could run out back and burn it, just to save some other girl from having to see it.

"Felicity?" a familiar voice asked from behind me.

I spun around to find Andy's mom at the next rack over.

"Oh, it *is* you," she said. "Hi!" she came over and gave me a big hug. At least she was still cool with me.

Andy watched us from behind the rack a few feet away, a deep frown on her face. "What are you here for?"

I swallowed, feeling nervous for some reason. I hadn't gotten a chance to tell her I was going to prom with Derek.

Well, it wasn't like she'd tried to talk to me, either. I wondered if she was here picking out a prom dress.

"I'm getting a dress," I finally said.

"Oh. Yeah, me too." Andy tucked her head back down and continued flipping through the rack.

Andy's mom looked back and forth between us. "Is something going on here?"

God, this was terrible. I felt like I was going to puke. Maybe I should just apologize. Was it really worth it for us to be so distant because of a guy?

She might even appreciate me making the first move.

I opened my mouth to speak.

"Mom, we need to get going," Andy said, turning away from

me. "I don't see any dresses here I like." She moved toward the front of the store.

Her mom shot me a sympathetic glance. "Bye, Felicity. See you later." She followed Andy out.

I sighed, all enthusiasm for prom dress hunting suddenly gone. Conflicting emotions poured over me—anger at Andy's continued stubbornness, guilt because I'd pissed her off to the point where we weren't speaking, loneliness because I wasn't close to one of my best friends anymore.

Would we ever be close again?

Mom popped up beside me, holding a long black dress covered in sequins. "How about this?"

I laughed. I couldn't help myself. "I'd look like Grandma in that."

She raised an eyebrow at me, about to say something, then glanced back at the dress. "Hmm. Yeah, I guess the shoulder pads are a bit excessive, huh?"

I nodded, my eyes sweeping the boutique. A sleek red gown caught my eye. I ran to it and held it up for scrutiny. It had two thin spaghetti straps on one side and a sophisticated side slit.

"Oh, Mom," I breathed. "I love it."

She studied it, her eyebrows pinched together in the middle of her forehead. "That slit looks a little high."

"Can I try it on? Please?"

After a long moment, she nodded. I dashed to the dressing room, then tugged my clothes off and slipped into it.

It fit like a dream.

I glanced at myself in the mirror. The dress was *made* for me. There was no way Derek could stay "just friends" if he saw it. It screamed sexy and glamorous.

"Well, come out!" Mom hollered. "I want to see it."

I stepped outside, holding my breath.

"Oh, it's gorgeous," she breathed. Tears welled in her eyes. "Honey, I can't believe how beautiful you look."

My throat closed up. As crazy as my mom could be, she sometimes knew just the right thing to say.

"Thanks."

"How much is it?" she asked.

Crap. I'd gotten so excited about it, I forgot to look at the price.

I glanced at the tag, the wind whooshing out of my lungs. "Two hundred and fifty dollars."

Mom coughed delicately. "Well, that may be outside your budget. Maybe we can find one like it for cheaper."

That was so not going to happen, and we both knew it.

I sagged my way back to the dressing room and changed into my boring clothes. Disappointment oozed from every pore of my skin. I wanted that dress so badly—and I wanted Derek to see me looking better than I've ever looked before.

I wanted him to see me as beautiful. Because if he thought of me as more than just a friend, I could be one step closer to winning his heart.

"So," Bobby said, eyeballing me, "do you have a date for prom?" He shifted in the chair at my kitchen table.

We'd decided to get together after school on Wednesday to work on our health class project. I figured it was easier to just have him meet me at home. I certainly wasn't going to meet him at the library, where Derek might see us and get the wrong idea. And I didn't really want to go over to his house, either.

I nodded enthusiastically in response to Bobby's question, thankful I wasn't available. What an awkward spot that would have been. Another minor crisis averted, thanks to my quick thinking. "Yup. I'm going with Derek Peterson."

His shoulders slumped. "Oh, I see." He chewed on the end of his pencil, staring at his notebook. "Just curious. I haven't gotten around to asking anyone yet."

"I'm sure you'll find someone."

"Yeah."

He looked so dejected, I felt a bit bad for him.

"Hey," I said in a cheerful voice, "let's figure out something really funny to do for our project. Have any ideas?"

He flipped to a page. "I already started thinking about it. Here are a few things I came up with."

I scanned the paper. Most of the ideas on the list were dumb, like making an instructional video or a health pamphlet, but one caught my eye.

"A game. That could be really fun."

Bobby perked up. "You think so?"

"Sure." My brain was going now. "We could do something to mimic the board game Life. Or like Monopoly. It could be really, really funny."

We worked hard for the next hour, bouncing ideas off each other. I had to admit, Bobby Blowhard wasn't actually that bad. He came off as a total dork in school, but when he wasn't around other people and trying too hard to impress everyone, he was actually pretty decent to be around.

After he left I threw my books upstairs and came down to help Mom with dinner. She was making meatloaf, my absolute favorite. My lovely brother was coming over for a midweek dinner, probably so he could filch some leftovers to take home.

"So," Mom said, cracking two eggs into the bowl of thawed meat, "I haven't seen Andy around lately. Everything okay?"

I shrugged, rinsing some potatoes off in the sink. "I guess. We're just fighting. No biggie."

"Well, I'm sorry to hear that." Mom ground the mixture in the bowl, then poured in some milk. "I saw her at the store last night with her mom. She seemed pretty mad, so I didn't say anything."

My throat clogged up. I grabbed a knife, parked myself at the table, and focused on skinning the potatoes.

"We haven't talked in days," I said, trying to keep my tone even. "She's gone boy crazy, and it's come between us." I sucked in a quick breath. "It's just not fair. She and I are supposed to be closer than that."

"It's hard when people start getting serious with a guy. It can make the other person feel left out. Maybe Andy felt a bit left out because of your attention to your new job, so she turned to her boyfriend."

I paused. I hadn't really thought of that before, but it was true. Since taking the job, I'd been obsessed with matchmaking . . . and repairing the effects of it.

And that included the Derek disaster.

Maybe Andy wasn't just mad about the cell phone incident, but about my distance as well. How odd that we could possibly be feeling the same emotions and not realize it.

I grinned. "You're a pretty smart cookie, Mom."

"Well, your dad seems to think so," she said, chuckling. She scooped the meatloaf into two glass pans, then popped them in the oven.

When I finished skinning the potatoes, I ran upstairs to my computer and turned on my monitor. I hopped into e-mail and composed a new message.

To: burgergirl@speedymail.com

From: dramaqueenie@emailmama.com

Subject: Sorry

Hey, it's me. Sry things R weird. Job's been stressful, and I know UR tight with Tyler. Also sry 4 hanging up UR cell.

That was not cool. :(

Hope we can talk soon. Miss you!

♥

Fel

There. I sent the e-mail and shut down my PC, feeling better than I had in days. At least I'd tried.

I studied for my trig test for an hour or so. Needing a break, I grabbed my PDA and scoured through my profiles so I could get more people out of love with Derek and in love with each other. I found another ten or so matches, so I made them and closed out of the profile document.

After that, I headed downstairs. It was finally dinnertime, and I was starving. The delicious scent of meatloaf had wafted up to my room.

I glanced around the kitchen, which was empty except for my mom. "Where's Rob?"

"He called my cell while you were upstairs. He can't make it tonight. Something about having to hang at the police station while some other officers are out."

"Well, I guess that's more meatloaf for me," I joked.

"I don't think so. I'm starving," my dad said, coming up behind me. I was surprised to see him home so early in the evening on a weekday. Workaholic and all that.

I gave him a hug. "Dad, I found the most gorgeous prom dress at the mall, but it was so expensive."

Mom swatted my butt with the hand towel. "Well, you're a working woman now. Save up that money! You can get it in no time."

"But I don't know if I'll be able to save that much in time," I said, my voice veering on the edge of whiny. "Prom's only a few weeks away."

"Your mom's right," Dad replied. "You can squirrel away enough money if you try. Or, if not that one, another that's just as nice."

Ugh. No sympathy from the parents at all. What a hard life I led.

Thursday morning before English class I searched for Andy in the hall and at her locker, but didn't see her. Nor had I heard back from her yesterday. Maybe she'd blocked me from her address book and wouldn't respond to my e-mails anymore. Great.

In a surly mood, I shuffled to my locker and dumped my backpack inside, grabbing whatever crap I needed for my next class.

"I heard the funniest rumor," a shrill voice said from behind me.

I whipped around to see Mallory talking to her friends Jordan and Carrie. They were all staring at me.

Double great. What a way to make a day even better—being taunted by the biggest jerk in school.

Jordan, chomping on a big wad of gum, replied to Mallory, "What did you hear? I wanna know!"

Mallory tucked a strand of golden blond hair behind her ear and said dramatically, "I heard Derek and Felicity are going to prom together. I never would have imagined it."

"Gee," I said, blinking as innocently as possible. "You know what *I* can't imagine? Why you're so concerned with what's going on in my life. Is yours just a little too boring right now? Or maybe you just don't have a date of your own for prom?"

She sneered. "Of course I have a date. I just wondered what the full story is. The only reason a guy would take *you* to prom is because he felt sorry for you, or because he was trapped into doing it." She tilted her head sideways and pursed her lips at me.

I felt a thud in my chest as my heart slammed hard. She didn't know how accurate that barb was.

"So," Mallory continued in a singsong voice, "I wonder which option applies here. Because you and I both know you're definitely not in his crowd."

"And again," I ground out through gritted teeth, "I wonder why you care so much."

My stomach lurched with irritation at being caught in yet another catfight with her. I was tired of her and her big mouth.

Mallory leaned in close to her friends and whispered, their loud giggles drifting.

Geez. Could she be more rude?

I shook my head in disgust, then darted away from my locker, glad to take the opportunity to escape. I tucked my head down and stared at the floor, slamming right into a huge back.

"Watch it," the guy snapped. I recognized him, though I didn't know his name. A football jock, hanging with the other cool guys.

"Sorry," I mumbled.

His friends stopped talking and stared at me.

"She almost knocked you over, puss," one guy said to the jock, his voice echoing down the hallway. Not an easy feat, given how many people were talking as they were walking to class.

Another guy with spiky brown hair eyed me. "Maybe you should try out for the team next year. You're pretty thick."

The guys started laughing hard.

A surge of heat flooded my cheeks. What an ass. This was quickly turning into one of those days I wished I could undo. Or go back to bed and stay there forever.

Derek came from behind them and slipped into the group. He looked superhot today in a dark blue shirt and jeans that fit him perfectly.

Please don't let them humiliate me in front of him, I silently prayed.

"Hey," he said, slapping one guy on the back. "How ya doing?"

Everyone's attention snapped to Derek, and the guys beamed at him, inching closer. I bit back a laugh. I hadn't thought about it, but even Derek's friends were affected by my matchmaking error. For a few more days, anyway.

"Hey, man," the spiky-haired guy said. "We waited for you so we could walk with you to class."

"Cool," Derek said. He noticed me standing in the group and shot me a smile. "Hey, Felicity. What's going on?"

My heart raced, and I swallowed.

"Nothing," I blurted out.

After all, what could I say? *Hey, Derek, I think you're a great guy, but your so-called friends made me feel like a fat, clumsy pig.*

"Oh, *hi*, Derek," Mallory said from behind me, sliding up to Derek's side in her teeny, tiny skirt.

My cue to leave. No way did I want to get into yet another fight with her when I was still recouping from the earlier one.

"Talk to you later," I said to Derek.

"Oh, okay. See ya!" He waved at me, then turned his attention back to Mallory and the rest of the group.

I took off down the hall to my next class, aware of how awkward I was, especially next to Mallory. Maybe she was right. As much as I was madly in love with him, as nice as he was to me, I didn't fit in with his group.

Not that I was a social outcast or anything. I had friends, and I got along with most everybody. But the jocks—and Mallory's fluffball friends, who usually hung all over those guys like a bad case of herpes—totally excluded me.

What bitter irony that Derek was in with them. Especially since he never treated me like an outsider.

I felt like he and I were Romeo and Juliet—destined to be kept apart because of awful circumstances and even more awful people.

It was just like Shakespeare. Well, other than the fact that Romeo actually loved Juliet back.

I stepped into English class and sat down, waiting for Maya to show up. I wished I could drown my sorrows in a pint of Ben and Jerry's. If ever an ice cream fix was needed, it was right now. Never had rocky road seemed more applicable to my life.

Chapter 12

"Hey," Andy said to me later that morning, nudging me in the back with her arm.

Startled, I spun around, slamming my locker closed.

"Oh, hi," I said as casually as possible, heart thudding in nervousness. I'd been starting to think she was going to ignore me forever.

"I got your e-mail," she said. "Thanks."

I nodded slowly, relief seeping through my limbs. It seemed we were making up, finally.

"Well, I feel bad things are so awful between us." I fixed my eyes on the hallway's speckled white tile floor. "I'm really sorry about what I did, Andy. I didn't mean to piss you off so badly." I glanced up at her.

"It's okay." She shrugged, giving a half smile. "Anyway, Tyler's busy during lunch. Maybe we can sit together and catch up."

Not the friendliest offer in the world, but at this point, I'd take it. "Sure."

We headed to health class together, carrying our stuff.

"You ready for our quiz?" I asked.

Andy nodded, twiddling a strand of hair with her free hand.

"It took me forever to get through that last chapter. It was massive, and so gross." I shuddered. "Those STD photos are nasty. So, what did you think about it?"

"Hmm? Oh, yeah, definitely a hard one to read." Andy glanced away and stepped into the classroom.

I got the distinct feeling she hadn't read the material. I parked myself in the seat beside her, then leaned over. "You sure you're all ready? Did you study last night?"

She pursed her lips. "Of course. Everything's fine."

Yup. She was so lying.

Andy is quite possibly the worst liar in the world, other than me. If they wrote a book on how to tell if someone is lying, it could be filled with the two of us. Andy always twitches her eyes funny and purses her lips in the same way when she's telling a big fat whopper.

I don't know what my giveaway tics are, but I'm sure I have them too.

I shook my head. "Okay, then." If she wasn't up for talking about it, I guess I wasn't going to force the issue.

Besides, if Tyler was at the root of the problem, I could see why she was hesitant to talk to me. I bet she'd spent every waking moment with him since our fight and hadn't studied at all. That was so not like her.

My stomach sank. This wouldn't have happened if I'd insisted we study together, like we normally do.

Or if I hadn't matched her with "babe" in the first place.

The quiz went by fast. Well, at least for me. Luckily, I'd squeezed in some study time in between staring at Derek under my eyelashes in the library.

As I wrote my answers, I kept sneaking peeks at Andy, watching her struggle. A part of me was tempted to help her, but I knew better. My luck, I'd get busted and thrown out of school for cheating.

The class bell rang. It was time to eat, thank God.

After telling Andy I'd meet her in the cafeteria in a few minutes, I grabbed my brown paper bag from my locker, then ran to the cafeteria as casually and coolly as possible. I'm sure I looked like a total dork who couldn't *wait* to eat her PB&J sandwich, but I didn't care. I needed to talk to Andy.

She was sitting at the corner table, our usual spot, with her iPod in her hand and her earbuds in her ears. No Tyler, just as she promised. Maya and Scott were already there, digging into their food.

I waved eagerly at the three of them and wove my way through scads of hungry freshmen to get to our table.

"Hey," I said, sitting on Andy's left side.

Maya gave me a quick, encouraging smile, then turned to talk to Scott. She knew Andy and I needed to have some talk time. I made a mental note to give her a big thank-you hug later.

Andy turned off her iPod and jammed it into her jeans pocket. "Hey, how's it been going, anyway?"

"Oh, fine." *Act casual.* "I've just been crazy busy the last few days, with work and school and all. You?"

"I've been busy too. Tyler and I are going to prom together, of course, so we're trying to figure out what to wear. I found a gorgeous gown, but it's pink, and Tyler doesn't want to wear a pink tie and cummerbund. But we're together, so of course we have to match, so I didn't buy that one. Anyway, the dress saga continues." She sighed dramatically, her eyes sliding to mine. "Soooo, when I saw you at the store a couple of nights ago . . . what's going on?"

I shot her a casual smile. "Oh, not much. I'm just going to prom. With Derek."

Her jaw dropped open, and she squealed. "Omigod, seriously?"

I nodded like an idiot, wearing a big doofy grin. "Yeah. But don't get too excited. We're only going as friends." I dropped my voice. "I just need to wear the absolute perfect dress."

That red one I saw in the store would be fabulous, if I could find a way to afford it. I'd only been a cupid for a couple of months, so I wasn't exactly rolling in the dough. Maybe I could put my paychecks aside and hold off on getting a cell phone, which I still hadn't managed to buy yet.

Andy squinted and tilted her head to the side, rubbing her chin. "Yeah, you need to look so hot that Derek can't resist you. He'll fall head over heels when he sees you."

"That's what Maya said. Obviously, I agree with that plan." My heart warmed as I shot Andy a big smile. Things felt like normal again, thank God. Even those few days of not being close were way too many.

I cleared my throat. "I just wanted to say, I'm sorry again about everything that happened."

"I know. It's fine. Let's just drop it, 'kay?"

"Sure thing." At this point I was so relieved to be on talking terms with her again, I would have promised just about anything. It didn't even matter that she never apologized to me.

"So, you wanna come over Friday night for a TGIF sleepover?" Andy asked. "I already asked Maya, and she's in. Ohhhh," she said in a breathy tone, "I can tell you the latest about Tyler and me."

"Sounds good." Not that I wanted to hear how much the two of them loved each other and probably wished upon a star every night for eternal happiness, but I could give a little. After all, people in love do bizarre things, right?

Like going to prom with someone just as a friend, in the small, desperate chance of making a romantic connection.

I guess I couldn't really be irritated with Andy. After all, at least Tyler returned her feelings.

"So," I said to Derek as casually as possible at our usual after-school meeting spot in the library, "what colors are you wearing to prom? I figured we could coordinate." I chewed more bite marks on the end of my pencil.

Desperate to push down my noninnocent thoughts about how

utterly attractive Derek looked today in his jersey and jeans, I figured I'd distract myself with my new favorite topic. Prom madness.

He looked at me with wide eyes, faking confusion. "I thought I'd wear black and white. You know, regular tux colors."

"Hardy har." I pointed my pencil at him. "You just don't understand girls. We put a lot of thought into this."

"Guys don't care about junk like that. So, Little Miss Prom Planner, what do *you* think?" He tapped his lower lip with his index finger. "Should I wear my azure blue vest? Oh, but what if I can't find the right shade of socks to match? The horror!"

I squinted at him in a mock glare. "Oh, a funny guy, eh? How'd you get so smart?"

"With a family as big as mine, you got to get attention somehow."

Oh, he'd never have to worry about that with me. I hung on his every word. During the past almost two weeks of hanging out, I'd gotten to know him better. Derek wasn't just a supreme hottie—he was smart and funny too. The ultimate combination.

I shook my head, amazed at how drooly I sounded to myself. *Loser.* No wonder Mallory thought I was a total dork.

I needed to stop feeling so desperate. Keeping cool was the

best strategy. Derek was trying to avoid crazy people, which was why he'd been meeting me in the library in between school and practice.

This was probably the last time we'd hang out like this. Because starting on Monday, he wouldn't need to hide out in the library anymore. The spell would be over, so Derek could stop having to find peace of mind in here with me. Great.

I tried to ignore the sinking feeling in my stomach. "Anyway, it's not a big deal about the prom colors. We can figure it out later." I glanced at my watch. "Oh, crap, I gotta go. I'm meeting Andy and Maya in a half hour."

The three of us, sans guys, were going to eat Chinese buffet at The Paper Lantern. I couldn't wait to pig out on General Tso's chicken, my absolute fav. But I still had to swing by my house to pack my clothes for tonight's sleepover, which meant I had to cut my library time with Derek short.

"Have fun! I'm gonna stay and finish my homework." Derek smiled, melting me into a little puddle of longing.

God, what I'd give to have him smile at me like that with more than just friendship on his mind.

The longer this whole saga went on, the more my heart ached.

Wanting to be in a relationship and being sooooooo close, but no cigar, totally sucked.

I hightailed it out of the library, ran home to pack, and met Andy and Maya in the nick of time, pulling into The Paper Lantern's parking lot with two minutes to spare. I ruled.

"Hey, girls," I said after I got inside the building. I slid into the red leather booth.

Maya gave me a big hug, whispering in my ear, "I think everything's okay now with Andy."

I squeezed her back. "Thank you so much," I replied, tears stinging the back of my eyes. She'd truly been a rock during all this drama.

Over the next two hours Andy, Maya, and I yapped like everything was back to normal. Andy talked about her dates with Tyler, but to her credit, she asked how things were going with Maya and Scott and about what was going on with me, too.

I dished about my overwhelming feelings for Derek, desperate to pick their collective brain about how to handle it.

"You need to play it cool," Andy said after chewing a mouthful of pork fried rice. She waved the chopsticks in the air as she talked. "You don't wanna freak him out like the school has with that superweird obsession going on."

"You are so right. Luckily, that'll go away on Monday," I said, nodding in agreement.

Maya, in the middle of drinking her Pepsi, stopped mid-sip, her eyes pinning me. "What do you mean? What's happening on Monday?"

Oh, crap.

Me and my big mouth.

Chapter 13

Ever tried to will your brain to think fast on command? Doesn't work.

I stared at Maya, trying to come up with something clever to cover my tracks. "Um, well . . ."

Yeah, great start, Felicity.

Andy raised an eyebrow. "Is there something you know that you're not telling us?"

"No. It's just that . . . I'm planning to let more people at school know Derek and I are going to prom on Monday, so they'll stop hounding him." Whew. Close call.

"Oh, okay," Maya said, nodding her head. "Good idea."

"Yeah, I guess that makes sense. I'll try to help with that too." Andy chomped down on another bite of rice.

I dragged in several slow, deep breaths to calm my heart rate. I really needed to be more careful about the cupid thing. One little slipup like this could cost me my job. And maybe next time I wouldn't be able to come up with a cover-up at all.

Conversation diverted, we finished up our food and headed to Andy's house, parking ourselves inside her room.

I was dying of curiosity and couldn't wait anymore. "So," I said as carefully as possible, "are you and Tyler getting any . . . closer?"

"He's so great," she gushed, grabbing a comb from her dresser and raking it through her hair. "We cut class the other day just to sit and talk in his car. He said he loves me so much."

Maya shot me a quick look of concern, then neutralized her face. "That's sweet that he cares so much about you," she said, plopping down on the floor and tucking her feet under her legs. "You two look adorable together."

"Yeah, that's really nice." I knew I sounded awkward, but I wasn't too thrilled to hear her admit to cutting classes. But calling her out on it would have been the worst thing to do. She and I were finally getting our friendship back, and I didn't need to blow it by telling her she was acting stupid.

"We're definitely ready to take our love to the next level," she said, braiding her hair into two thick plaits and wrapping a ponytail holder around the ends. "Tyler's band is playing at a party tomorrow night. I think it'll happen right after that."

"*It?*" I asked, afraid to have her clarify, but wanting to make sure I understood. I fiddled with the ends of my own hair, trying to appear calm and rational and totally nonjudgmental so Andy wouldn't get mad at me.

"*It.* You know. Sex." She dug into her drawer, pulling out her pajama pants.

Maya sucked in a quick breath. "Wow."

"Well, I hope everything works out the way it's supposed to," I said. "And that you two are . . . safe and careful." There, that was generic and supportive sounding. I mentally patted my own back.

"Thanks, you guys. And don't worry, we'll use condoms." Andy beamed at me. "I'm glad we're not fighting anymore, Felicity."

For once I could tell her the straight-out truth. "Me too. So, whose party is it?"

"Jenny's. Hey, do you two wanna come with me? She told me to bring some friends."

I weighed the options. Sit at home and worry about Andy making hasty, spell-induced choices, or go and have the chance to maybe talk her out of it. Plus, I could do some matchmaking research while I was there. A total no-brainer.

"I'm there," I answered.

"Want a beer?" a wasted jock said from behind me. His words slurred as he sloshed a red plastic cup toward my face. He smiled as he looked me over, his eyes watery and unfocused. "You look thirsty."

As he moved, light amber liquid jumped over the side of the cup, splashing onto the carpet.

Luckily, I dodged out of the way, preventing the beer from splashing onto my clothes. My mom would kill me if she thought I was at a drinking party, and coming home smelling like a brewery was a surefire way to get locked up in my room forever.

"Um, no thanks." I held up the full cup of soda in my hand. "I'm good."

I turned away from him and rolled my eyes in disgust. If anyone needed a health class list of nondrinking activities to do at a party, that guy did.

Maybe I should recommend a few ideas to him. Mrs. Cahill would be so proud.

"Whatever." The drunk guy ambled across the living room, squeezing through the crowds, presumably headed out back to where Tyler's band was playing.

I mean "playing" in the loosest sense of the word, of course. Now that I'd actually had a chance to hear them, I quickly realized how much I disliked being subjected to cover after cover of whiny emo songs.

Andy, of course, ate it up. She'd insisted on all of us grabbing lawn chairs and parking right in front of the band. But after hearing five songs of Tyler's overenthusiastic drumming, I'd taken a break from the music to grab another soda.

I think Maya and Scott were happy I did so, because they'd hightailed it after me. We'd been people-watching in the house for the last several minutes, checking out the hookups . . . and giggling at the guys who were being denied.

"Okay, that guy's totally going to be ditched by that girl he's talking to in less than five minutes," I said, pointing toward a couple in the corner of the room. "Just watch."

Scott laughed. "You're probably right. He already spilled his beer all over her pants. That's a great way to win a girl over."

"Yeah, you know that would work for me," Maya said with a snort. She took a sip of her soda.

The guy in question, a sophomore at our school who apparently did not know how to hold his alcohol, was gawking with bleary eyes at his date's chest, like he wanted to grab hold and never let go. He was a good six inches shorter than she was, so his gaze hadn't risen above her chest more than once or twice as he'd rambled on and on.

Poor girl. That had to be no fun. Not that I'd ever had anyone leer at me like that, but I could just imagine the awkwardness. Bobby was bad enough with the hard-core flirting, but at least he'd never blatantly stared at my boobs.

"So," the guy said in a loud voice that carried to our side of the room, "what're you doin' later tonight?" He pressed the palm of his free hand on the living room wall behind her, pinning her in.

The girl noticed where he was staring and glared at him, crossing her arms in front of her. She mumbled something, glancing around the room.

"Aw, come on," I heard him groan. "Who cares where they are? I'm right here."

"Aaaaand here's where she makes her grand exit," I said, sitting back triumphantly. "She's looking for an escape right now."

"Good call," Maya said, snickering. "She's desperate to get away."

The girl gestured as she talked, then ducked under his arm and took off running up the stairs.

Now alone, the guy sulked off toward the kitchen. Likely, to refill his beer cup . . . again. Because that was a great idea.

I did not envy the hangover he was going to have tomorrow.

"Well, that was fun. I'm gonna go find Andy," I said to Maya.

She nodded, slipping her hand into Scott's. "I think we're gonna stay in here," she said. "It's much nicer."

I gave her a quick hug, then stepped outside. Dusk was starting to fall, so I wanted to find her before it got too dark to see. I didn't recognize some of the people here, but most were from our school.

Jenny had a huuuuuge house. One of the most popular girls in our school, she was always throwing parties when her parents were out of town—not that I'd been invited before, but I'd heard all about them. Her backyard stretched on for over an acre. Which was good . . . and bad, considering how many red plastic cups littered the lawn. She was gonna have a fun time cleaning up the mess tomorrow.

I just hoped her parents, who weren't due back from their vacay in Aruba until tomorrow night, didn't decide to return home early.

I noticed Mike, a guy in my American History class, sitting all by himself on a lawn chair. He was busy pulling handfuls of grass out of the ground. Maybe I needed to give him something else to occupy his time. Like . . . a new love match!

I looked through the crowd until I found a candidate for him. Wendy, a girl I knew from anthropology, was standing against the fence with a couple of her friends, checking her watch every minute or so and gripping her cup in her other hand. She looked utterly bored too. That was one thing they had in common, anyway.

I grabbed my PDA and sent them love messages. Not ten seconds later, both of them grabbed their cell phones and flipped them open, nearly simultaneously. Then their eyes glazed over and they rubbed their chests.

Wendy handed her cup to her friend and wove through the crowd to Mike.

"Hey," she said, licking her upper lip. She gave him a wink.

"Hey yourself," he answered back, staring at her mouth. "Whatcha up to?"

"Not much."

Next thing I knew, she was perched on his lap in his chair, running her fingers through his hair as they kissed.

Ah, another blissful match made. Hopefully, they wouldn't go too crazy with the public displays of affection . . . or private. The last thing I needed was to be responsible for a wave of teen pregnancies during the next nine months.

On that sobering note I put my LoveLine 3000 away. Time to do what I'd come outside for—find Andy.

I spotted her near the front, still in her lawn chair where I'd left her, and made my way to her side.

"Hey," I said loudly.

"Oh, hi!" she yelled back over the sound of the music. "I'm glad you made it back. Did you bring me a Cherry Coke?"

I smacked my forehead. "I'm sorry. I completely forgot—some idiot was getting on my nerves and almost spilled beer on me. I'll go grab it."

She rose from the lawn chair. "Nah, it's okay. I'll get it. Here, save my seat."

I sank into the chair, watching Tyler spin his drumsticks as he jammed into another drum flourish. I didn't remember this particular song having a percussion solo, but hey, what did I know?

"Tyler's rockin' that drum set, huh," a husky voice said in my ear, sending goosebumps across my skin.

I glanced up to see Derek beaming at me.

"I didn't know you were going to be here," I said, standing up. My eyes soaked in the sight of him.

"I didn't, either. Just decided to come at the last minute. I couldn't miss Tyler's big gig, you know."

I laughed, glancing at the band. "So, what do you think of them?"

He shrugged. "Not too bad."

"Not too good, either," I joked.

His teeth sparkled in the dusky light. "I wasn't going to be the one to say that."

Someone pushed by and jostled Derek into me. He grabbed my arm to steady himself, and before I realized what I was doing, I boldly pressed up against him, taking advantage of the moment.

We froze, me staring up into those beautiful eyes of his. I felt like I was drowning.

I saw him swallow, and he leaned his face closer down to mine, his mouth mere inches away. "Felicity, do you—"

"Derek!" some guy said, popping up from nowhere. "Hey, man, want a drink?"

I groaned as Derek pulled away and turned his attention to the intruder. Why was it we couldn't get more than a few sentences into a conversation without someone interrupting us?

Derek nodded. "Um, sure." When the guy took off, Derek shrugged at me. "Who am I to pass up a free butler, right?"

I laughed. "If I'd known you would be here, I would have loaned you mine. Jeeves does so love to serve."

He raised an eyebrow at me, chuckling. "How thoughtful of you."

The song ended. Tyler's voice rang through the speakers. "Thank you! We're gonna take a quick break."

The lead guitarist added, "We'll be back in a little bit, after the groupies get drunk."

The crowd laughed.

Jenny darted to her stereo, pulling up a playlist on her iPod to keep the music going, then headed toward the band. When she passed us and saw Derek, her face broke out into a broad grin.

"Oh, I didn't know you'd be here!" She hugged Derek tightly.

Jealousy clutched my stomach, and I tried to push the feeling down. He wasn't mine to be green-eyed over.

"Can I get you something to drink?" she asked him.

"Actually—" Derek started.

"No, I insist. You stay here. Don't move." She took off toward her house, sashaying her curvy figure.

Derek laughed. "I guess I'll just stay here, then."

Andy returned and chatted with us for a minute. Then Tyler appeared out of nowhere by her side, and she shot him a loving glance.

"Hey, baby," she said, winding her arm through his. "I was hoping to have some time with you." She dropped her voice and gave him a meaningful look. "Alone."

Crap! I ordered my brain to think of a stalling tactic, glancing desperately around the backyard for inspiration. If I could keep her outside until Tyler had to play his next set, maybe she wouldn't do ... *it.*

"Hey, did you hear the news about ... Wendy and Mike?" I said, referencing the couple I'd paired up a few minutes ago, who were currently still going at it on his lawn chair.

She paused, her interest obviously piqued. Andy loved a good story and always was the first to know about anything, but since being with Tyler had eaten up a lot of her recent time, she wasn't as current.

Even Derek looked curious, his eyes fixed on me.

"No, what about them?" Andy asked.

"They're all over each other like white on rice," I said to them, pointing in the couple's direction. "Looks like one wild and crazy hookup." I paused, an idea formulating in the back of my brain. "And I bet there will be more tonight, if we all hang out together and watch for them." Hell, I'd make matches all night, if that's what it took.

Andy cast her eyes between me and Tyler a couple of times. She chewed on her lip, considering her options, then said, "You and Derek have fun. I'm gonna hang with my baby for a little bit."

Before I could say anything else, she and Tyler took off inside the house. I watched them go, hoping against hope they weren't ducking up into a bedroom to do the nasty. As tempted as I was to stay right on her heels, I didn't think it was the best idea for me to follow them. Now that would be *really* nasty.

"I'm sure it's fine," Derek said to me, his low voice warm and comforting. "The house is packed with people."

I looked back up at his eyes. "How did you know what I was thinking?"

"Your face is pretty easy to read." He gave me a crooked grin. "I can tell you're worried about Andy. She's smart. It'll be okay."

I swallowed. If he could read my thoughts that well, who knows what else he'd read on my face? Did he know how deeply in love I was with him?

I felt heat crawl up my throat and sneak across my cheeks. I was grateful for the darkening sky, which hopefully hid my embarrassment.

Derek's "butler" came back, thrusting a cup into Derek's hand. "Here ya go," he said, grinning toothily. "Hey, wanna go shoot some hoops? Jenny's brother has a basketball net set up in front of the garage."

"Thanks, but—" Derek started to say, but was interrupted by Jenny, who jumped between the two of us.

"Derek, here's your . . ." She trailed off when she saw the drink in Derek's hand. Her mouth turned down in the corners. "Oh. You already have one." She paused. "Well, do you want to see the kitchen? I can show you where it is." Her eyes raked over Derek, and she smiled, running a finger across her lower lip. "Or I could always give you a tour of the house."

"*Or*, we could play some hoops," the guy said, shooting Jenny a glare.

She glared back at him. Then both turned expectant faces toward Derek.

He coughed, shuffling from one foot to the other. "Well, actually, I need to find the bathroom. Where—"

"Here, let me show you," Jenny said, grabbing his arm. "Follow me."

Jealousy reared its ugly head again, this time stabbing me in the stomach. I sighed. This worship over Derek was getting to be a bit too much. I needed to break away before I did something really stupid.

"Okay, you guys have fun. I'm gonna head out." I glanced at my watch. "Gotta be home early anyway, or my mom will kill me."

Derek nodded, but he didn't look too happy. I wished it was because I was going. "Okay then."

Jenny tugged on his arm, pulling him toward the house.

Well, I wasn't happy, either. I was getting damn sick of watching people fawn all over him. And it's not like I had any right to say anything.

I was only a friend, after all.

"See ya," I said, heading back through the house to the car, stopping only to say good-bye to Maya and Scott. While I loved Derek, I wasn't going to be just another groupie.

At least I had my dignity. Cold comfort that it was.

Chapter 14

I spent the earlier part of Sunday fretting obsessively about Andy. I tried calling her cell several times, but got no answer. No doubt she was too busy—*ick*—to call me back. I didn't even want to think about what she and Tyler were doing together.

Tyler was an okay guy, but after getting to know him these past two weeks, I wasn't as fond of him as I was at the start (unlike Maya's guy Scott, whom I'd grown to like more and more, especially since he and Maya were so good together). And I definitely didn't like the side of Andy that Tyler was bringing out.

Tyler was way too immature for Andy, and his clinginess only made Andy superclingy too. Not exactly what I had in mind for my BFF when I made the match. Yes, if Andy really loved him, of course I'd be supportive of her choice, but there was no way to tell if it was true love until after the spell wore off. I wished Andy wouldn't make this huge decision before then—it was just one more day!

I closed my anthropology book, unable to focus on the reading. *Please still be a virgin,* I prayed silently about Andy. It was my fault things were like this, and I couldn't let that feeling go.

I mean, what if she was too love-blind for condoms, and she got pregnant, or got an STD? She'd end up one of those single moms on a cheesy made-for-TV movie, and I'd be the "best" friend who led her astray by introducing her to love.

I logged on to my PC and set a blog entry for private.

I'm so worried about Andy right now. She hasn't called me back. She's dropping everything for Tyler. It's almost like an obsession.

How could the love spell make her this crazy, that she's rushing to do . . . it, after two weeks?

Should I keep trying to call her? Should I go over to her

house and see what she's doing?

I stared at my fingers resting on the keyboard, realization hitting me square in the face. This was totally not what friendship was about. I was trying too hard to control her relationship—which wasn't mine to control.

And even more, my "help" wasn't wanted.

Andy needed my support and friendship, not me trying to enforce what I felt was best for her. After all, if Derek returned my feelings the way I wanted him to, I'd probably be wrapped up in dating him, just like Andy was with Tyler. Was it fair for me to be so high and mighty about everything, when I didn't know how I'd be in the same situation?

Maybe it was time to get back to the heart of the matter—that friends support one another, no matter what.

I erased what I'd written and replaced it with new text:

I solemnly vow to support my friends, regardless of

whatever choices they make. Because friends do that for

each other, and I'd want them to support me.

I saved the entry, feeling worlds better about my decision. Of course, it didn't take away all of my anxiety. But it was a good first step.

Monday morning I scanned the courtyard in front of the school, looking for Andy. She was there, waving frantically at me.

I darted over, pulse galloping like mad. *Stay cool,* I told myself. *Remember, you're here to support, not control.*

"So . . . how are things going?" I asked her. "Have you been busy? I didn't hear back from you yesterday."

"Things are fine. Sorry, I was swamped." She leaned in closer. "Tyler's grandma got sick while we were at the party on Saturday, so we didn't get a chance to . . . well, you know. Cement the deal."

"Oh, for real?" I struggled to keep the excitement out of my voice, even as I mentally vomited at the awful image she painted in my mind. "Well, I'm sorry to hear that about his grandma."

The bell rang. We headed down the pathway, where Maya joined us just inside the front doors. We moved to a less trafficked area of the hall and stopped to talk.

"You look tired," Andy said to Maya. "You been sleeping okay lately? Or are you too busy with Scott to sleep?"

Maya gave a small smile, swatting Andy on the arm. "Things have been a bit crazy lately around the house. You know how it goes."

Hmm. Now that Andy mentioned it, Maya did look a little different. She still pretty much acted the same, but I'd noticed her face was more . . . drawn lately. I remembered her heated comments about *The Scarlet Letter* from before.

"What's going on?" I asked Maya. "You *have* been off lately."

She sighed. "My parents have been a bit hard on me because I'm spending time with Scott. All they do is gripe—with me, and with each other. They want me to study instead of go on dates."

"That sucks. I'm sure they want you to do your best, but it's not like your grades are a problem or anything," I offered.

Andy nodded sagely to Maya. "I feel your pain. It's hard when you're trying to make a relationship work, and you don't feel support from your family."

I swallowed, guilt washing over me. "Or friends," I said meekly.

Andy hugged me. "It's all in the past now. Things are looking better." She paused. "Besides, now we all have dates for prom and can go together. How cool is that?"

The three of us yapped about prom for a couple of minutes,

with Maya telling us all about the gorgeous black prom dress she'd snagged this past weekend. I'd pretty much given up on my dreamy red gown, so it was time to look elsewhere for something a little cheaper. I only had a hundred bucks or so saved from my job, and even if I got bonuses from all my latest matches for lasting, I'd still not be able to buy both the dress and shoes in time for prom. Plus, there were other expenses that went along with it: dinner, boutonniere, and so on.

As we talked, I glanced around the hall, sensing a distinct mood change in the air. No longer was everyone gushing about Derek.

In fact it was unusually quiet, only whispers flitting through the air. People didn't scour the halls looking for him, but pushed through with heads down, as if embarrassed to be seen loitering around.

I heard one guy at his locker mutter, "Derek's cool, but he's not as amazing as I thought."

Caren, a brunette I knew from last year's English class, nodded thoughtfully at his words. She looked at him offhandedly, then gazed at the guy's face again, like she was really seeing him for the first time.

Sucking in a deep breath, she twirled a lock of hair around her finger, pushing out her chest a bit to catch his attention.

Oh my God, she was totally flirting with him. And I hadn't even gotten to pairing her up with someone else yet. She'd gotten over Derek on her own.

It worked! The spell was gone.

I glanced over at Andy, who didn't seem any different, given how much she'd talked about Tyler this morning. So she still had the hots for him, regardless of their spell wearing off. Her relationship with Tyler was here to stay, then.

I bit back the disappointment. If I wanted her to be a friend to me, I'd have to be a friend to her and support her, even if she continued to be annoyingly in love.

Maya and I parted ways with Andy and headed into English class. We slid into our seats, busting out our copies of *The Scarlet Letter* for today's discussion.

"Settle down," Mrs. Kendel barked to the class, shooting all of us a glare. She closed the door with a heavy thud.

Everyone zipped their lips fast. She was obviously in a mood, and when Mrs. Kendel was mad, it was a good idea to stay quiet.

"Okay, let's finish up our discussion on *The Scarlet Letter*. There's a part in the book," Mrs. Kendel said, flipping through her well-worn copy, "where Hester's daughter Pearl asks if she will be getting a scarlet letter of her own when she's older. What do you think is the reason she asks? What's the main purpose of this scene?"

Everyone stared silently at Mrs. Kendel. Yeah, it was totally Monday in here.

Maya raised her hand.

"Miss Takahashi," Mrs. Kendel said, "go ahead."

Maya cleared her throat. "Um, I think since the letter represents sin, that maybe Pearl wonders if she's going to sin as a grown-up, like her mom has?"

Mrs. Kendel blinked rapidly, obviously surprised. "That's exactly it."

"Though . . . Pearl could also be making a point about judging others," Maya continued, getting more impassioned as she spoke. "And that really, no one person is better than anyone else. And holding people to standards *you* think they should be achieving is totally unfair to that person."

I glanced at Maya, whose cheeks flamed red. She clamped her mouth shut, leaning back into her seat.

This stuff with her parents must be bothering her more than she's let on. I'd never seen Maya rant like that before.

"That's absolutely true," Mrs. Kendel said, not noticing how upset Maya looked. "In reality we all sin, so we all bear a scarlet letter."

I scrawled out some notes on what Mrs. Kendel was saying, but I had a hard time focusing. I definitely needed to talk to Maya about what was going on with her.

And soon.

Later that morning Andy and I strolled through the hallway to health class.

"So anyway, I didn't get a chance to tell you earlier, but I finally bought *the* perfect prom dress," Andy said, bouncing in excitement. "It matches the dark purple of Tyler's cummerbund perfectly."

"Awesome. Derek teased me when I tried having the conversation about matching outfits," I said.

Out of nowhere Tyler appeared in front of us, stopping us in our tracks.

"Hey!" Andy gasped, then leaned over to kiss him on the cheek. "I was just talking about you. I hadn't heard from you at all this morning—what's going on?" Deep lines etched in her brow. "Is your grandma doing any better? She didn't have to go to the hospital, did she?"

He glanced away and dug into his back pocket, handing her a note. "Uh, look, Andy. I need to run, but I wanted you to read this."

"Sure."

He turned and left. Andy's eyes followed his rapidly retreating figure down the hallway.

"Well, that was weird," I said, trying to cover up the uncomfortable moment. "Maybe he was just in a hurry."

She nodded, opening the note and scanning its contents. Her face fell, and tears welled in her eyes. "Oh my God," she said, pressing her free hand to her mouth.

"Are you okay?"

Wordlessly, she handed me the note.

I scanned its contents, biting my lower lip as I read. "I'm so sorry," I whispered to her.

She sniffled. "I can't believe he broke up with me, Felicity. And in a stupid note! How could he do this?"

Startled by her raised voice, students turned and glanced at Andy's burning cheeks.

"Come over here." I pulled her aside. "We have a couple of minutes before class starts."

Hands shaking, Andy squinted away the fresh tears in her eyes and began to read the note out loud. "'Babe, I've been thinking about this a lot.'" Andy looked up, scoffing. "Right. Breaking up with his girlfriend though a freaking note? Sounds like he put a *lot* of thought into this. And he sure didn't sound like he was thinking about dumping me last night when we were talking on the phone."

I rubbed her back, my stomach lurching from Andy's pain and my own guilt. I couldn't tell her that last night, he'd still been under Cupid's spell. "It's okay. I know you're pissed."

"Believe me, I am. And hurt." She glanced back at the note, continuing where she left off. "'I don't think this is gonna work between us. It's going too fast. I need some more space. Let's just be friends.'" She scoffed. "But this part is the most unbelievable: 'I hope you'll still come see our band perform on Friday. Tyler.'"

I shook my head in disbelief. "What a total jerk. He obviously didn't deserve you."

The whole scenario floored me. I hadn't even thought of the possibility that the spell could wear off Tyler but not Andy, since Andy was clearly more amazing and Tyler didn't deserve her in the first place.

I felt like such a heel. I'd tried to help her find love, but all I did was set her up to get hurt, and in such a callous manner.

Andy crumpled up the note, fire flashing in her eyes. She dumped it in a nearby garbage can.

"We'll get through this," I said. "Don't sweat him. You're too good for him anyway."

We headed back down the hall to health class, Andy alternating between being supremely pissed off and supremely hurt. In one moment she cussed him up and down, then cried in the next about how she'd been wrong to let herself be vulnerable with him.

She stopped suddenly outside of the classroom door, her mouth flying open in shock. "Oh my God, I just realized I don't have a prom date now. What am I going to do? I already bought a dress."

Crap, crap, crap. The suckiness of the situation just kept piling up. With the drama about him breaking up with her, I'd forgotten all about prom.

"We'll figure something out," I said. "I promise."

The idea of pairing Andy up with someone else came to mind, but I pushed it away just as quickly. It was way too soon. Besides, I didn't want her to just go through this heartbreak again.

I had to do something to make this better, though at the moment, I was fresh out of plans.

Chapter 15

Bobby, who never had good timing, accosted me right before the bell rang for health class to start. Today he had on a shirt that showed his midriff, but at least it wasn't see-through.

I guess that could be counted as progress. Baby steps, right?

"Hey," he said. "Thought about which board game we want to mimic? That needs to be turned in next Monday, right?"

I stepped around him and headed to my seat, knowing he'd be following me closely. "Yup. We should figure that out."

He slid into the seat beside me, nodding eagerly. "How about tonight?"

"Well, I have a work meeting, but maybe we can meet afterward."

Andy slumped into her chair, swiping a hand across her red-rimmed eyes. My heart broke for her. "Hey, Bobby," she muttered.

Bobby waved at her. "Hey. I was just talking to Felicity about our health project. We're working together. As a team. Just the two of us."

I bit back a groan. God, could he be any louder about it? Why didn't he take out an ad in the school paper while he was at it?

"Let's definitely get together tonight, Bobby, okay?" I needed to shut him up, so maybe placating him would do the trick.

A few minutes into class Andy slipped me a folded scrap of paper. I furtively opened it, pretending to take notes.

Fel,

Haven't worked on project yet. Maybe Cahill will let the 4 of us work together? My partner's James.

Actually, that could work. It would save me from more alone time with Bobby, at least. And maybe James would mention how things were going with him and Mitzi. It had been a couple of weeks since I'd paired them, but I'd barely had a chance to observe them together, seeing as how Mrs. Cahill wouldn't let them change seats and sit beside each other in class.

Plus, I could help Andy make up some of the schoolwork she'd missed while salivating over Tyler.

I scrawled an answer:

Sure. We'll ask after class. L8r!

We approached Mrs. Cahill after the bell, ready to beg, if necessary. But she was surprisingly receptive to the idea, though she specified we were all to pitch in and help with the project.

Art class at the end of the day confirmed that things were basically back to normal. Students weren't hovering around Derek's table. In fact, a few people—including the teacher—completely ignored him. But Derek seemed relieved to have breathing room.

I tried to act casual, but couldn't keep my eyes off him. What if he decided he didn't want to go to prom now that he could find another person to go with as a friend . . . or something more? I was torn between asking him outright and just letting it slide.

After the final bell of the day rang, I scooped up my stuff and headed to the library to study.

Okay, I went to wait for Derek, even though I suspected he wouldn't show up. After all, for him, the library sessions were about hiding from the adoring crowds, and now he didn't need to do that.

But by now, I had to be honest and at least admit to myself that *I* didn't care about studying. It was really about spending time with him. Seeing his face at the end of school always made my day. I was just as in love as ever, but that love was deepened by a closeness we didn't have before.

Not that I could fess up to him about any of it. I still had to play the "best buds" role to keep from scaring him off.

Derek came in just a minute after me, a huge smile on his face.

"Did you see?" he asked as he slapped his backpack on the table. "Things are back to normal."

I nodded. "I'm sure you're happy about that."

"Absolutely. Now, I don't have to keep hiding out in here. What a relief."

And just like that my world came crashing down. What a kick in the gut. Who was I kidding? Only myself, apparently.

I was nothing to him. Never would be.

Throat tight, I gave him the biggest fake smile I could muster, gathering my books and cramming them in my backpack. "That's great. I guess we can stop hanging out now. I'm sure you're ready to have your afternoon back."

Derek gave me a funny look. "I guess."

I needed to leave before I started crying in front of him. "Well, I'd better run. I'll see you around, okay?"

I swept past him and, once I'd fled the library, let the tears spill freely down my cheeks.

As soon as I got home from school, I grabbed a pint of Ben and Jerry's ice cream from the freezer, then dug around in the silverware drawer and snagged a spoon. This was no ordinary depression. This was full-fledged, I'm-in-love-with-a-guy-who-only-wants-to-be-a-friend-or-maybe-just-a-friendly-acquaintance depression.

The worst kind, if you ask me.

Maybe there was no sense in trying with Derek. All this time, I'd thought getting closer to him would show him how good we'd be together. And all he was thinking about was how he didn't want to be in hiding anymore.

Great job, Felicity.

Over the course of my cupid employment, I'd managed to

butcher nearly every match I'd made, including the ones for both of my best friends, as well as my own pathetic attempts to endear myself to Derek. I sucked at my job. I sucked at my life. Yeah, I'd pretty much hit the ultimate low.

The only thing that could make things worse would be to find out I was really born a boy or something.

A few minutes into feasting on my comfort food, I heard Mom's key in the front door. She strolled into the house, whistling a little tune.

"Oh, hey," she said, then stopped midstride, eyeing me chowing down on Chunky Monkey. She hung her keys on a hook, put her purse on the table, and sat across from me. "Bad day, huh?"

I nodded and swallowed hard, my throat closing up. "Things just aren't going right for me at all anymore."

She stared at me for a moment, then got out of her seat and went upstairs. A minute later, she came back down, a long bag in her hands. The curve of a clothing hanger peeked out the top.

"What's that?" I asked.

"Just open it and see." Mom had a mysterious smile on her face.

I slid the bag off, gasping when I realized I was holding a red dress. My dream prom dress! Mom had gotten it for me.

My eyes blurred, and tears slipped down my cheeks. "Oh my God. Thanks, Mom. This means a lot to me."

She smiled bigger. "We were going to wait and give it to you later, but you looked like you needed a pick-me-up today."

I squeezed her in a tight hug. "Yeah, that sure did it."

She hugged me back. "You still have to get your own shoes and accessories," she said, "but your father and I wanted to do something special for you. We know you've been working hard at your job and school lately. And you really did look gorgeous in it."

I slipped the bag back over the dress. Was this fate's way of telling me not to give up? Maybe the dress was a sign that I still had a chance of winning Derek over.

I dashed upstairs and hung up the gown in my closet, then grabbed the phone and started punching in Andy's number. I paused. She probably wasn't in the mood to talk about prom stuff, seeing as how she and Tyler just broke up. It was tempting to call Maya's cell, but I knew she was at band practice.

Well, it was time to go to my meeting with Janet anyway, and then hurry home so I could help plan the health project with Andy, James, and Bobby, who were all coming to my house tonight.

I borrowed Mom's car and drove to Cupid's Hollow headquarters.

Once I got inside, I darted into Janet's office, breathless as I plunked myself down in the seat.

"Sorry," I said, trying to relax and look professional. "It's been a crazy day."

Janet raised a perfectly arched eyebrow. "I see. So, how go your matches? If I remember right, the big spell should have worn off by now."

I nodded, slightly awed at Janet's incredible recollection powers. I wasn't sure how many cupids were out there, but she must have had hundreds, or even thousands of matches to keep track of. And I could barely keep on top of the ones I'd matched myself. "You're good. Yeah, the spell ended last night, and fortunately, it seems like everything's back to normal."

"That's good. Be sure to watch your other matches closely, though," she said, eyes fixed on mine in a warning stare. "You don't want them to go down the drain while you're focusing on repairing the damage from this accident. It's too easy to lose control."

I swallowed and handed her my PDA. "Yeah, I made a lot of couples over the last two weeks." I paused. "I did have a . . . person who was still in love after the spell wore off, but the other person fell out of love."

Janet sighed. "That's a real risk of the job." She plugged my LoveLine 3000 into her computer, synching it with the master program. "It's unfortunate when that happens. The best you can do is try again."

Yeah, I *could* try again in the near future. With Andy, I mean, not with Tyler—I was so pissed at him, it wasn't funny. No way could I make an objective match for him right now. But when would Andy be ready?

"How do you know when someone's ready to be matchmade after they've broken up?" I asked Janet. Maybe she could help give me tips.

She pursed her lips. "I wish there was an easy answer, but each person's different. Some are ready to jump right back into love, while others need to heal for a while. That's why it's good to take your time and make the best quality matches you can."

I nodded solemnly, trying to ignore the light, nervous fluttering in my stomach. The rapid matches I'd made weren't exactly the highest quality . . . but they sort of mostly met the minimum compatability requirements and the initial chemistry seemed pretty strong, so surely the odds of them working out were on my side. Right?

Janet handed me back my PDA, as well as my paycheck. "Next

week we'll see how your other couples are doing. Meanwhile, check and double-check your e-mails before you send them, just in case."

I stood. "Thanks again for your help."

"Anytime."

"That's dumb." James crossed his arms and sulked. "Games are stupid."

For the two hundredth time in the past five minutes I clamped my teeth down on my lower lip to keep from yelling at him. Next to me at the table Andy was about to have convulsions from rolling her eyes so much, and I didn't blame her. James was being a total pain in the ass to deal with.

"Well, unless you have a better idea, that's what we're doing," I said.

One eyebrow raised, I waited for a minute while James glared at me.

"No?" I asked. "Great."

Bobby shuffled through some papers on the table until he found the one he was looking for. "Here's a rough sketch of what I thought we could do." He handed me the paper, a dark blush working its way over his cheeks.

Aw, he was embarrassed over offering his ideas. Probably not too comfortable being around Jerky James, knowing anything and everything was fodder for mockery.

I glanced over the paper Bobby had given me, then paused in surprise. It was actually quite clever.

"Hey, this isn't bad!" I exclaimed. "I like how you made our game look like a Monopoly board."

Andy eyeballed it over my shoulder. "Oh my God, this is too funny. Look, you made 'jail' into a VD clinic!"

We both giggled.

Bobby shrugged, a shy smile on his face. "Just trying to help."

"Don't be so modest." I looked him over, suddenly seeing him in a new light. He was much smarter than I'd given him credit for. "This is really good."

Andy whipped out a pencil and started marking on his paper. "We can set up each of the squares to be hot dating spots, or different places around the city."

James kept pouting.

"Well, if we're having a VD clinic, a pharmacy should go on here too," Bobby said. "Maybe the pharmacy can be the 'free parking' space for the game."

"I like that idea," I said to Bobby. "You did a great job with planning this out." He'd taken the brainstorming ideas from our last session and followed through with them in an effective way.

Maybe he wasn't so horrid and obnoxious after all. He just needed to be in his element, which was apparently a small group setting.

Bobby glowed under the praise. "Well, thanks!" He tucked his head near Andy's, and they pored over the paper as she wrote.

By the end of the session we'd split up the duties for who would work on what. James was going to create the figurine pieces, Andy would make the money and property cards, Bobby would handle creating the board, and I'd craft the outer box.

The only thing left was to vote on the name.

"I vote for my idea of Crabble," Andy asserted, leaning back in her chair and crossing her arms in satisfaction. "That one makes me giggle every time I think about it."

"But that's dumb. It makes you think of Scrabble," James pointed out, "which isn't the kind of game we made. This is a Monopoly board."

"Who cares?" Bobby said. "I think it works too."

I glanced at him in shock. I'd never seen him stand up to other guys like that before. Bobby usually asserted his masculinity through severe fitness workouts, not by running his mouth or standing up for himself.

Or for anyone else, for that matter.

"I like Crabble too," I said to James. "That makes it the majority vote. Besides, I didn't see you coming up with anything. If you're going to keep shooting down all of our ideas, at least come up with something else."

Man, he was totally annoying. One of those guys who didn't like anyone else having funny ideas, because he couldn't get the glory for it. Thank God we were now far enough along to not have to work with him as closely anymore.

Honestly, I couldn't tell what Mallory had seen in him when they'd dated freshman year. But that reminded me—I wanted to ask him how the love was going with Mitzi.

I quickly thought up a way to ask about her as slyly as possibly. "Hey, James, who is Mitzi paired up with in health class? Do you know what she's doing for the project?"

Instantly his demeanor softened. I'd never seen anything like it—especially considering the love magic was already gone. This was genuine emotion I was seeing in him, possibly for the first time ever.

A soft smile played on his lips. "She's working with Mary. They decided to do a poster. Speaking of which, I gotta run." He flipped open his cell phone to check the time. "We're studying together tonight."

Andy, Bobby, and I watched him go.

My chest ached with the bittersweet irony that I'd actually made a decent match for a guy I couldn't stand, but Andy, one of my best friends in the world, had gotten messed over because of my poor matchmaking on her behalf.

And not only that, I'd screwed things up for myself as well. Surely I'd end up alone, in an old Victorian house with eight hundred black cats all named Mittens, hosing down kids who walked across my lawn. And when I died, they'd find my bones propped up in a rickety rocking chair, wearing my red prom dress—

"Hello, earth to Felicity." Andy waved her hand in front of my face. "You still here with us?"

I blinked rapidly, shaking away my morbid thoughts. "Yeah, sorry. Zoned out there for a minute."

Andy and Bobby glanced at each other, a knowing look passing between them. I guess they were both used to dealing with me by now. I offered them a chagrined smile.

"Actually, I gotta run too," Andy said, packing her stuff in her bag. "I need to study." She sighed deeply, the corners of her mouth turning down, and I knew she was thinking about Tyler and missing him.

"It'll be okay," I said, giving her a big hug. "You're better off now."

Tears pooled in her eyes, and one slid down her cheek. "I know. But I just miss him. I can't believe it went like this."

Bobby nodded. "Breaking up is hard. That was lame of him to dump you in a note."

Andy and I stared at him, jaws dropped.

"How did you know what happened?" I asked.

He shrugged. "Everyone at school knows. Sorry."

Andy started sobbing, fat tears plopping onto her shirt. "Great. And I'm a laughingstock now too!"

"No, you're not. They're all saying what an ass Tyler was." He awkwardly patted her on the shoulder.

She sniffled and swiped her hand across her eyes, glancing at him. "Really?"

"Yup. Everyone knew you were too good for him anyway."

Wow, Bobby was proving to be a pretty decent guy. I appreciated the way he was trying to comfort Andy. I think it helped her to hear these things from other people, not just me.

"Thanks," I said to him.

He gave me a small smile, then turned his eyes back to Andy. "No problem. No problem at all."

Chapter 16

"Okay, Jon. Why don't you start? Tell us what's going on from your point of view." I shifted in the booth and took a sip of my iced mocha latte.

It was Tuesday, and we'd decided earlier this morning that Starbucks was safe, neutral ground for Jon and Megan's after-school couple's therapy session.

He drew in a slow breath and kept his eyes on his coffee. "Well, I think Megan's great, but she's a little too . . . gung ho about this weekend trip to the cabin. To the point where she's—"

"Gung ho?" Megan yelped. "If you love me, I should be more important than golf."

"I don't think going to one golf game means I don't care about you," he rebutted.

"Okay," I said. The last thing we needed was for things to get too heated. "So, you guys are afraid your . . . values don't align with each other's. Good start." I paused, considering my next words carefully. "Is it possible to find a compromise you can be happy with?"

Megan sniffled, then took a drink of her chai tea. "I just can't compromise on this. I need all of him, not just whenever it suits his needs."

Jon blinked. "I want to play golf. It doesn't mean I don't care. I just don't want to be pushed."

Poor guy. I could kind of see his point. Megan was being surprisingly stubborn about this. I'd never known her to act in this way. Of course, I'd never dated her, so maybe her attitude with guys was way different.

Megan glanced at Jon, then looked away, her eyes following a guy with his arm wrapped around a girl. The guy kissed the girl on the top of her head, drawing her closer.

"See that guy?" Megan asked, nodding her head in that direction. "Look how he's nurturing her. You can tell she's important to him."

Jon's jaw clenched. "Well, if I'm so terrible, go find a guy like that."

"Fine." Megan stood, swiping her chai tea off the table. "This is ridiculous anyway. You're obviously wrong for me. I need someone who puts me first every time. We are over."

My mouth flew open in shock. I instantly regretted matching Jon up with her. And the shock on his face as she walked out the door was like a kick in the nuts—or would be if I had any.

Jon gripped his cup so tightly I was afraid it would crush beneath his hands.

I struggled for a moment with what to say. Then, an epiphany hit me. Actually, Megan was right. Trying to counsel them to stay together *was* ridiculous. If the match wasn't right in the first place, I couldn't and shouldn't force them to work things out with each other.

"Well," I finally said, "I think you're better off. She's on crack if she thinks any guy in his right mind will deal with that attitude for long."

Jon stood, giving a pinched smile. "No kidding. I'm outta here."

I wanted to hug him, but I didn't think it would be a good idea. So I nodded my head and said, "I don't blame you. And for what it's worth, I'm sorry."

Jon smiled in earnest this time. "Hey, thanks for trying."

o   o   o

The rest of the week flew by rapidly, and before I knew it, it was already Friday. I sat in art class, unable to tear my eyes away from Derek, who was studiously working on a paper mosaic. He'd been friendly as usual toward me since Monday, but without our after-school library sessions, things weren't the same, and I basically tried to avoid him. I was feeling the bitter sting of his absence and missing him terribly.

Junior prom was a month away. I needed to find a way to get closer to him before then. But how?

Luck, it seemed, brought the answer to me. After the bell rang Derek popped over to my desk.

"Hey," he said. "How are you?"

My heart thudded in my chest. "Fine. You?"

"Not bad." He gave me a crooked smile. "Just working and stuff. So, how's your job going? Have you done any matchmaking yet?"

We strolled out of the classroom and down the hall at a casual pace. "Well . . . ," I stalled, weighing my words carefully. One slip could do me in. "I'm just keeping busy right now in the accounting department."

In a way it was true—I'd been counting nothing but unhappy couples all over the place.

Yes, it seemed I was quite possibly the worst matchmaker in the world. My best effort hadn't helped squat with hardly anything. My pairs were splitting up left and right. That morning, on the way into school, I'd seen two couples break up right in front of me.

It was a class-A disaster.

But I didn't want to focus on that right now. It was time to change the subject. "So, prom's coming up soon," I said in a shaky voice, staring at my feet as we walked.

"Sure is. Did you find your pumpernickel dress or whatever? I don't remember what color we'd decided on."

I laughed. "Lucky for you, it's plain red."

"Works nicely. I have black and white everything. The downside is, I look like a waiter at The Burger Butler." He shifted his backpack higher on his shoulder as we passed through the school's front doors.

"I'm sure you'll look great. Probably better than poor Andy looks in one. She's a server there." An image popped up in my head of Derek wearing a tux, his broad shoulders accentuated by the cut of the suit jacket.

Oh, God, he was going to look so. Freaking. Hot. It would take all of my willpower not to throw myself on him and beg him to love me.

"What's on your mind?" he asked.

"Um, nothing." Nothing I could repeat anyway.

I glanced around in front of the school and saw Andy just a few feet away. She waved at us and dashed over.

"Hey, Felicity. Oh, *hi*, Derek," she said, a sly smile on her face.

Oh, God. Please don't let her spill the beans about my mad love for him. I sent her a message through my brain waves: *Don't you dare embarrass me!*

She waved me off with a small hand movement, as if my concerns weren't valid.

"So, I hear you're taking Felicity to prom." She squinted at him. "Getting to be good friends, aren't you two?"

"We sure are," I butted in, trying to nip the conversation before it could get underway. I couldn't sit there and listen to Derek talk about what a great bud I was, or how I was probably like one of the guys to him. "So, Andy, you ready to head out to my house? We need to wrap up our health class game."

That was actually true—the projects were due on Monday, so we were going to finalize our presentation plans before our TGIF sleepover tonight and make sure all of our elements were completed in time.

Derek snickered. "I remember doing that. Have fun." He waved and strolled off around the corner, like he didn't have a care in the world. Especially not a care about me.

I groaned, wishing I could bang my head through the school's brick walls.

"This is pure torture, Andy!" I cried out. "I'm never going to get him to see me romantically."

"Hey, at least you get the chance to be in a romantic environment with him. Prom's your opportunity for love. My date ditched me." Andy's shoulders sagged, and her smile slid off her face. "This sucks."

My gut twisted. I felt like such a heel. Here I was, going on and on about my problems, when Andy had a truly crummy situation.

"I'm sorry. If you want, I'll hang with you that night instead of going to prom. We can rent a few bad movies and pig out on Chinese."

She looked at me, tears in her eyes. "You'd do that for me? You'd give up your one romantic moment with Derek?"

I nodded rapidly. I truly meant it. Andy and I had had our ups and downs lately, but she was still my best friend.

"Absolutely," I said. "Friends come first. Always."

She hugged me tightly, and I heard her sniffle. "I should have put my friends first while dating Tyler. I'm sorry."

"It's okay," I replied. And it was. "Sometimes, falling in love is like . . . being under a spell."

"It sure is," she said, pulling back and swiping a hand across her damp eyes. "Anyway, I don't want you to give up your prom date."

"Thank God," I laughed, "because my dress is so hot. I don't think you could appreciate it in the same way a guy would."

She laughed and slugged me in the arm. "Hardy har. Funny one."

A brilliant idea hit me.

"Hey, you should still go with all of us. Derek and I are just going as friends, anyway. Unfortunately." I gave her a mock grimace. "Seriously, though, we could all hang out. It would be a blast. You could be Derek's other date. He'd feel like a total pimp, having two hot mamas on his arm. I wouldn't want you to waste your prom dress, either."

"Thanks, but that's okay. I don't need to be a third wheel. Maybe I can find another use for my prom dress, like mopping the floor or something."

I saw her bite back a sigh and paste on a big smile. I couldn't believe she wasn't going to go. Prom wouldn't be the same without Andy.

Chapter 17

"So, like, chlamydia would be terrible to catch. As would pretty much any sexually transmitted disease. They're totally gross." Mitzi opened up her huge trifold poster for everyone to see. "Just to reinforce this, I pasted in lots of pictures to show you guys."

The dozen or so images she'd glued onto the poster board were horrific. Fortunately, several of them were bad photocopies, so I couldn't make them out. But the ones I could see were just wretched.

The whole class gagged in near unison. I had to look down at my paper for a moment to keep from ralphing on the desk. I could hear Bobby retching slightly from right behind me. It was weird that he wasn't sitting on my other side for once, but he probably just wanted to keep our group closer together. With Andy to his left and James behind her, we could have almost passed for a unified team.

Even Mrs. Cahill blanched and gave a slight shudder. "Um, nice job, Mitzi and Mary. That was very . . . informative."

Mitzi beamed, folding up the dreaded poster board and tucking it under her arm. She slid back into her seat. "Thanks!"

Most of the presentations had been pretty clever so far. One group made an instructional video of dating scenarios on how to tell your potential partner if you had herpes, complete with what worked and what didn't.

We all busted up into fits of laughter for nearly five minutes over the film—especially the part where the girl was explaining to her "date" in a posh restaurant downtown that you didn't catch herpes by sitting on a toilet.

Even better, in the background of the restaurant you could see all the patrons who were trying to eat dinner, eyes wide with shock over the subject matter. I couldn't believe they'd actually filmed on location.

Mrs. Cahill actually had to smother a laugh behind her hand at that one. You know, she wasn't too bad, actually. Considering the subject matter she was teaching, I guess she made the best of a crappy situation.

"Next up are . . ." Mrs. Cahill looked at her list. "Bobby, Felicity, Andy, and James. They all worked together on their project. Come on up, guys."

Stomach twisting in nervousness, I grabbed my piece of paper. My job was to explain our project, while the other three would "model" the pieces.

"Well," I said, exhaling slowly and trying to keep my hands from shaking, "we decided to create a board game about STDs called Crabble."

The class interrupted my speech with fresh peals of laughter.

I gave it a moment, then continued. "We made ours like Monopoly, though you'll probably never see a game like this in stores. And that's too bad, because it's both fun *and* informative."

For the next ten minutes we explained the ins and outs of Crabble, with Andy and Bobby doing a great job of showing the workings. James pretty much sat there and did nothing except trade flirtatious looks with Mitzi. Of course.

Oh, well—I didn't care. He'd helped make the game, so he technically did carry his own weight. I was just ecstatic to be done dealing with him. And thrilled that he and Mitzi were still going strong. At least *that* match hadn't ended in heartache and disaster. And if they stayed together long enough, I'd get a nice bonus in my paycheck that I could put toward the perfect boutonniere for Derek, and new makeup to complement my dress.

When the presentation was over, we got some great applause. I went back to my desk feeling good about how that went.

I slid a note to Andy:

Nice job! Glad that's over.

She wrote back:

Srsly. Total relief! Another stress off our plates.

After she handed the note to me, I saw her turn back to another piece of paper, scribble something on it, then fold it up and hand it to Bobby.

What the . . . ?

I heard him snicker from behind me, then the scratching of a pencil as he replied to her note.

During the rest of the class period, I pondered the note-passing. What was going on with that? I'd never seen the two of them talk before. It was great to see Andy in a good mood again, though she'd gotten a little weepy when the subject of Tyler came up during our TGIF sleepover. But Maya and I had both been relieved and impressed by how well Andy held up for most of the weekend. I knew she was still sad about what happened with him, but she seemed more like her old self by the minute.

Suddenly, I had an epiphany: Bobby realized how important Andy was to me. In order to help me see what a great guy he was, he was talking to her and helping her feel better after the Tyler fiasco.

Not that it was going to make me date him, but I could totally appreciate the new side of Bobby. He was growing less obnoxious and more tolerable to be around. In fact, he was rather thoughtful.

Feeling like I'd reached a new peak of enlightenment, I strolled to my locker after class to fetch my lunch, then headed to the cafeteria.

Andy and Bobby were already there, the board game in front of them. They were pointing and laughing at some of the places on the cover.

I had to give myself kudos too—I really outdid myself with the box design. It was sheer genius.

Okay, the genius was Bobby's with his brilliant idea, but I totally came through on my part.

Andy waved me over. "Hey, girl! We were just talking about how great you did with the box. It's hilarious."

Bobby nodded enthusiastically. "It's one of the best parts of the whole project. You rock."

I shrugged modestly and slipped into the seat across from them. Good old Bobby—he could always be counted on for an ego boost. Guess he was just that kind of guy. It was tragic, really, that I didn't like him more. I could see how he was pretty cool, if you looked past the mesh shirts.

Actually, he wasn't even wearing a mesh shirt today. In fact, his top didn't show any part of his abdomen or muscles at all. Interesting. Either Bobby was working harder to impress me, or he was "dressing up" for the presentation.

Well, whatever the reason, it was a refreshing change. It made me not embarrassed to be around him.

"Thanks. That was fun," I answered.

I dug out my requisite PB&J sandwich from my lunch bag and started chowing down. All that hard work and thinking had sure made my appetite spike.

After lunch I told Andy I'd see her in class, then darted to my locker. I'd completely blanked on bringing my anthropology notebook with me.

I opened the lock and rifled through my backpack.

"Hey, Felicity," a low voice said from behind me.

I spun around. It was Derek. Of course, my heart did its typical jump-into-my-throat action.

I forced myself to relax. "Oh, hi, Derek. How are you?"

If looks were an indicator, I'd say he was doing mighty fine. Yowza, he looked extra hot today in a green T-shirt that made his eyes seem piercing.

Or was it the look he was giving me? I'd never seen Derek staring at me so intently before.

He swallowed, then shot me a crooked smile. "I'm on my way to lunch, but I wanted to ask you a quick question. What are you doing tonight?"

"Uh, nothing. I don't have anything going on this evening," I blurted out in a rush. I hoped that didn't make me sound like a total loser, but it was true. No study date tonight, and my meeting with Janet had been postponed until Wednesday because she had to go out of town unexpectedly. "Why, what's up?"

"Well, I was wondering . . ." He paused, clearing his throat. "I wanted to know if you'd like to come over for dinner tonight."

"Who, me? At your house?"

"Absolutely," he said, chuckling. "My mom wants to meet you, since we're going to prom together."

Oh my God. Meeting Derek's parents?

That was kind of a big deal, wasn't it? I mean, even though Derek and I were going as friends, it still was a good idea for me to make a favorable impression on his family.

"Sure, that'd be great," I said.

He paused, looking like he was going to say something else, then glanced at his watch. "Oh, gotta go. I'll pick you up at six thirty, okay?"

I nodded mutely, watching as Derek's fine figure strolled away. What a crazy, crazy day it had been so far, and I had a feeling tonight was going to be just as interesting.

The rest of the school day went torturously slow. But once I got home Mom kept me busy cleaning around the house, so evening came surprisingly fast.

In my bedroom I finished dressing and stared at my reflection in the full-length mirror. My hair was softly pulled up on my head, with small tendrils curled around my face, and my dress was flattering to my figure, but provided full coverage for modesty. I needed to make a good impression on his family, and looking like one of my brother Rob's hoochie dates wasn't going to do that.

As I glanced at my feet, clad in cute sandals, it hit me that Derek would finally have a chance to see my painted toenails. At that moment, staring at my toes, the full impact of going to dinner at Derek's house hit me.

Oh my God. I was getting ready to embark on the most important moment of my love life with the guy of my dreams.

The breath whooshed out of my lungs, and I dragged in a deep gulp of air, trying to calm myself down. *Chill,* I ordered myself. This was not the time to put pressure on myself. *Remember your mantra of cool and casual.*

I grabbed my purse and headed downstairs, stepping carefully so I wouldn't take a header and break my neck. Because that would totally be my luck.

Mom and Dad were reading on the living room couch. Mom glanced over and gave me an approving nod. "Oh, honey, you look lovely. I wish you'd dress up more."

"Thanks, Mom," I said, giving her a wobbly smile.

"He's going to be bowled over, I just know it," she said. "Remember your manners, because his family will be watching every move you make."

Crap, she was right. They would be watching me, sizing me up.

As I continued to think about it, it started to seem that my entire life and possible future happiness was riding on tonight.

Oh God, oh God, oh God. I was going to be sick.

Mom eyed me, a deep frown line between her eyebrows. "You okay, Felicity?"

I nodded slowly, sucking in air. I needed to stop psyching myself out, stat. This was ridiculous. It was just dinner, not a meeting with the Pope.

"I'm okay," I said, ordering my pulse to steady itself. "Just nervous."

"Don't be," Mom replied. "You're gorgeous. Derek would have to be blind to not see that."

The doorbell rang, and Dad got up to answer it.

Derek strolled through the door, and my knees buckled. He shook my dad's hand, said hello to my mom, then looked at me.

"You look great, Felicity." He shook his head with a smile.

"I mean, you always look nice, but you look great today." A light flush swept up his throat and across his cheeks.

Was he nervous too? My heart rate sped up again. I managed to thank him, though my throat was closed so tightly, I don't know how I got the words out.

"You ready to head to my house?" he asked.

I nodded. "Absolutely."

We zipped down the road in his car about a mile, ducking through side streets and making small talk, until we pulled into the driveway of a nice-size house. Well, it would have to be with that many kids.

Derek got out of the car and came to my side, opening the passenger door for me. What a gentleman!

I hoped against hope my body wasn't shaking visibly, because my insides felt like boiling butter.

He opened the front door and ushered me in. Giggles echoed throughout the living room, and I heard scrambling sounds. A stuffed animal flew through the air and smacked against my stomach.

Derek's jaw dropped. "Hey! Who did that?"

The sounds stopped. A blond boy, who had to be in kindergarten, stepped out. "Sorry," the boy said to me, his eyes cast down. "I was aiming for Derek."

I ruffled his hair. "It's okay. There's no internal bleeding or anything."

A woman's voice came from another room. "Derek? Is that you?"

Another wave of nervousness came over me. It was time to meet Derek's folks.

Chapter 18

A blond woman with delicate features rounded the corner and stopped, patting a hand to her chest. Her stomach was huge and round, so I guessed she had another bun in the oven. I remembered what Derek had said about his parents loving kids. Obviously, he wasn't kidding.

"Oh!" she exclaimed, her eyes sweeping over my face and figure. "You're even prettier than Derek said!"

Derek talked to his mom about me? And he'd told her I was pretty?

In shock, I turned to look at him.

"Mom, *please* stop it," he said.

"It's okay," I replied, trying to make him feel better. "After seeing you, my mom told me what a hunk she thinks you are and how cute we are together."

His cheeks turned red. When I realized what I'd said, I could feel mine burning too.

Hey, way to keep digging that grave for yourself, Felicity. Maybe next time I could just show him my top secret blog posts and save myself the trouble.

Luckily, his mom intervened. "Felicity, we're having fried chicken and baked potatoes. I hope that's okay." She glanced at Derek, then looked back at me, a twinkle in her eye. "Derek loves my chicken, so I made a few extra just for him. He has a hearty appetite."

"Mom," Derek said in a low voice, swiping a hand through his hair. I don't think I'd ever seen him so flustered.

"Sorry, honey." She hugged him, then hugged me. "I'm glad to finally meet you," she whispered in my ear.

"I'm glad to meet you too," I whispered back, smiling. She was a really nice lady. I could see why Derek was so cool, with a mom like that.

"Okay, you guys get the kids settled in the dining room. We'll bring the food in," Mrs. Peterson said.

Derek escorted me toward the dining room, his hand on the

small of my back. I could feel his warm fingers through the fabric of my dress and fought the urge to turn around and lean against him.

I took the free seat across from Derek, between two of his siblings. They all looked the same, including Derek, just with varying ages. It was so cute.

"Mommy, I'm staaaarving!" the teddy bear thrower, Sam, cried out. He grabbed his fork and thumped it on the table in beat with his words. "Chic-ken legs! Chic-ken legs!"

Derek shot him a stern look. "Stop that, or I won't let you watch the robot movie tonight."

That did the job. The boy stopped midcry and put his fork down, folding his hands in his lap and giving an angelic smile. "Look, I'm being good now, okay?"

"And you're doing a great job at it," I told him, deadpan. "My brother's four years older than me, and he doesn't behave *nearly* as well as you do. He's a bad boy who gets in trouble all the time."

"Really?" he asked, eyes wide. "Does his mommy spank him?"

"Not nearly enough," I answered, giggling.

Mrs. Peterson entered the room, holding a big glass pan of chicken in her gloved hands. Derek's dad followed her closely, carrying the baked potatoes.

"That smells great," I told them. "Thanks again for inviting me over."

I looked over at Derek to find him looking at me, his face unreadable. A hot flush swept over my cheeks, and I prayed I hadn't sounded dumb.

Dinner was a louder affair than I was used to, but lots of fun. I managed to get through the entire meal without any nervous vomiting, so that was good. After talking to Derek's parents, I could totally see where he got his wit, and his warmth. They had plenty of both.

The only thing that made me feel a little nervous, actually, was Derek himself. I'd catch him staring at me sometimes, like he had something on his mind, but he never said anything. He kept the conversation light and fun.

Was I hallucinating things, or maybe reading into his looks because I wanted to believe he was interested in me? It wouldn't be the first time I'd misread a situation.

After dessert, I thanked Derek's parents for the great meal, hugging his mom and then shaking his dad's hand. Derek ushered me into his car, and we rode back to my house in mostly silence.

"My parents really like you," he finally said as he pulled his car into the driveway. "They wanted me to let you know you're invited over to our house anytime. And Sam wants you to come back over and watch the robot movie with him."

I grinned, bending over to grab my purse from the floorboard. "That's nice of them."

I sat up, and our eyes connected for a long moment. I glanced at Derek's full lips. Would he try to kiss me?

I jerked my eyes away. This wasn't a date. We were just friends. Having these fantasies about him was just going to ruin a good evening. I didn't need to put myself in a position to make things awkward between us . . . or even worse, embarrass myself.

"Thanks again for having me over," I said. "I had a great time."

His lips slid into a smile. "It was my pleasure."

I walked to school Tuesday morning, eager to dish to Andy and Maya about how dinner went yesterday. I'd spent the rest of the evening lying on my bed and staring at the ceiling, replaying the dinner through my head over and over. I'd been tempted to call them, but I knew Maya was on a date with Scott. And Andy was helping her mom with her mom's latest woo-woo obsession.

In some ways I couldn't believe how well the night had gone.

As I walked down the sidewalk, I replayed all the information I'd gained, ready to dissect it with the girls.

One, Derek had touched me several times on the hand and lower back. Definitely a good sign.

Two, he'd told his mom that I was pretty . . . unless she was saying that just to be nice. No, she didn't seem like that kind of person.

Three, dinner was great. No awkward silences. Just casual, fun conversation. And even better, his family liked me.

But four, no signs of a kiss or irrefutable signals that I was anything more than a friend in Derek's eyes. One through three meant I *could* be—but he might also just be an affectionate pal. I needed Maya's and Andy's advice on how to find out for sure.

I came through the school's front doors and stopped dead in my tracks. Almost a quarter of the students in the hallway had a sullen mood that permeated the atmosphere. People were moping down the hallway with deep frowns on their faces. I even saw a few girls crying.

I spotted Maya near her locker, kissing Scott on the cheek. He left, and she waved me over.

"Hey!" she said, then glanced around. "Actually, I probably shouldn't be so perky on a day like today. It seems like the whole school is in a bad mood."

"I wonder why." I paused, then said in a low voice, "Oh, no, did someone die?"

"—such a jerk," I heard one girl say as she walked by, her voice wobbly. "He just dumped me out of the blue, saying he couldn't understand what he'd seen in me for these past two weeks."

Oh, crap. The picture suddenly cleared up, and I realized what was wrong—and whose fault it was.

A massive chunk of the love matches that I'd made two weeks ago in a fit of matchmaking fury had worn off . . . and apparently, for the worse.

My stomach sank clear into my feet, and I groaned out loud.

"What's wrong?" Maya said, concern etched in her face. "Did something bad happen between you and Derek too? It seems like everyone is griping about love lately. It must be something about prom season."

I shook my head. "No, Derek and I are fine. Confusing, but fine." I grabbed her elbow. "We'd better head to English. I'm betting Mrs. Kendel won't be in a good mood if we make her wait."

Besides, I'd paired Mrs. Kendel up with a fellow teacher, and considering the way so many people looked horrible and depressed, odds were she would be too.

Class seemed to drag on forever. Almost everyone kept quiet, their downturned faces reflecting their bad moods. Mrs. Kendel seemed crabbier than usual, doling out an essay assignment for us to work on in silence during the class period. She sat behind her desk, a perpetual frown on her face as she glared at all of us.

I felt sick to my stomach, knowing I'd wreaked more havoc.

Perhaps I shouldn't have made those hasty matches after all. If I had just waited for my original love spell to wear off the whole school, there might have been a lot less heartache all around.

Well, give yourself another brownie point, Felicity, I grumbled to myself. *You screwed up. Again.*

I finished writing the world's worst essay and handed it up to the front of the aisle. Well, that was a fun waste of time. I'd been so distracted trying to figure out how to fix the matchmaking problem that I knew I totally blew the assignment.

The rest of my morning classes were more of the same—mopey students everywhere. Fortunately, it wasn't everyone. There were a few couples I saw who actually looked in love still—a few that I'd matched, and several that must have found love on their own. At least I hadn't messed up everyone's lives.

Maybe I needed to stay out of the business of love, both in my professional and personal life. I should just give up on Derek, give up on being a cupid, and go back to being plain old Felicity. No pressure, no stress. No risk of hurting people . . . or being hurt.

I made my way through the hall toward health class and got an unexpected glimpse of Derek. He was with a group of his friends.

"Hey, man," one of his football friends said, thumping him hard on the back. "Did you see that game last night?"

"Nope, missed it," Derek replied, slugging him in the arm.

Guys. If I lived a million years, I'd never understand the draw to pain.

"There was this amazing shot you should have seen," the guy said. "I'll tell ya later about it."

His friends took off in one direction, and Derek kept heading toward me. We locked eyes, and he smiled, the dimple deepening in his cheek.

I melted, and all the embarrassment of my mismatched matches faded away. I was so, so crazy for this guy. Who was I kidding? I couldn't stop loving him any more than the sun could stop rising in the east, or the moon could stop causing the tides.

Hell, I couldn't even stop myself from making sappy metaphors about how much I loved him.

"Hey," I said, hoping my feelings weren't all over my face. "I had a great time at dinner last night. Tell your mom—"

"—and the cashmere sweater was on clearance, since they're getting rid of their winter stock," a loud voice said from behind me. But not just any voice.

Of *course*.

I bit my lower lip and rolled my eyes, willing myself to relax. I could get through this.

Mallory and three of her giggle-box friends moved beside me. "Hey, Derek," she said, her eyes raking over him, then me. "Oh. Felicity. What are you doing?" The question itself was innocent, but her tone implied I didn't have the right to be around him. God, you'd think I was hanging out with Derek just to torture her or something.

"I'm heading to class," I said, my tone snippier than I wanted it to be. I hated letting Mallory know she got the better of me.

Her jaw tightened for a quick moment. Then she relaxed her face into a smarmy smile and glanced at her friends.

The four of them continued down the hallway.

"See ya," Mallory said to me over her shoulder.

As they walked off, I saw their heads close together. One of the girls peeked back at me, shaking her head.

Great. I just loved being talked about by stupid, snotty girls. I hoped Andy would show up soon. She'd know what to say to make me feel better.

"I'd better go," Derek said, shifting a book higher between his arm and side. "We'll talk more in art, okay?"

"Yeah, that'll be good."

I waved bye to him and made it to health class. Andy arrived right as the bell rang, so I didn't get a chance to talk to her about the dinner date at Derek's house. And Mrs. Cahill kept us busy.

I swear, everyone was conspiring against me today.

When the bell rang, Andy grabbed my arm. "I gotta talk to you," she said.

"Oh my God, me too," I said, happy I'd finally have some uninterrupted time to talk to my BFFs at lunch.

"Felicity," Mrs. Cahill said. "Can you come here a second?"

I closed my eyes and breathed in deeply. "I'll be right there," I answered Mrs. Cahill. I told Andy, "Go ahead and wait for me in the cafeteria," then went to talk to the teacher.

"Felicity," she said, perching on the edge of her desk, "it's about your project."

"Yes?" I asked, trying not to sound too nervous.

She smiled. "Nothing bad, I promise. Your group board game was really, really clever. I'd like to bring it to a continuing education class I'm participating in, as an example of good health class activities."

"Really?" I was floored. She actually thought it had merit.

"Absolutely. It was creative and fun, and made a dull topic more interesting."

So she knew we were all bored to tears. Well, at least she was trying to spread the love and help other health class teachers keep from boring *their* students.

"Sure thing," I said. "I'll bring it back to school tomorrow."

She dismissed me. I flew to my locker and grabbed my brown bag. Carrying my lunch, I went into the cafeteria, spying Andy at a table, her back facing me. She was leaning over and whispering in a guy's ear.

She laughed, and he turned to face her, a huge smile on his face.

Holy crap. Andy was talking that closely with . . . Bobby Blowhard?

Chapter 19

I walked as calmly as possible over to Andy, tapping her on the shoulder. "Andy? What's . . . going on?"

She whipped around in her seat, gasping when she saw me. "Oh, Felicity!" She stood up and hugged me, then sat back down, her face beaming. "I was trying to talk to you earlier. I wanted to surprise you. Bobby and I are going to prom together!"

The oxygen rushed out of my lungs. Whoa, I was certainly not expecting that.

"Well, you sure did surprise me," I said slowly, taking a seat beside her. I glanced at Bobby's beaming face, then looked the rest of him over, taking in his nice, completely non-see-through shirt.

Bobby saw me evaluating him. A flush spilled over his cheeks, and he dropped his gaze to his twiddling fingers.

"I knew Andy was depressed about prom," he explained. "And I already had a tux in my closet from my older sister's wedding last summer, so I asked if she would go with me."

"Wasn't that sweet?" Andy's eyes flitted back and forth between me and Bobby. "He didn't want my dress to go to waste. And since we had fun working together on the Crabble game, we figured it would be fun to hang out. Plus, we were each gonna sit at home alone anyway. Now we can triple-date with you and Maya!"

I squinted and stared at Andy, who was babbling like crazy. She seemed edgy, her fingers playing with the strap of her purse. Why would she be so nervous, unless—

I mentally smacked myself on the forehead. How could I have missed the signs?

1. the notes passed back and forth
2. sitting together at lunch
3. Bobby taking a sudden interest in Andy, which

   I'd always thought was because of his interest in *me*

God, how vain was I? I was a class-A idiot. Bobby and Andy were crushing on each other. I didn't know when he got over me, but he sure did, with full force.

Some matchmaker I was—apparently, my love radar must be permanently broken.

The irony of the situation struck my funny bone, and I started laughing hard until tears streaked down my cheeks.

Andy stared at me with a weird look on her face. "Did I say something funny?"

I wiped the tears away. "No, no. Sorry. I just realized some stuff. I guess I've had my head stuck up my own butt for a while now." I looked at him, then her. "I didn't see you two getting . . . closer."

Andy bit her lower lip. "So, you're not mad at me?"

"Are you kidding?" I smiled. "I'm just glad to see you happy."

"Well," Bobby said, "I'm sure you guessed that I used to have a small crush on you." He slipped his hand into Andy's. "But then I realized Andy is the one for me. I hope I didn't hurt you or anything. Don't give up on those dreams of finding someone special just because of me, Felicity."

I almost started laughing again, until I realized he was dead serious.

Keeping my face as straight as possible, I said, "Thanks. I'm a pretty strong girl. I think I'll make it."

Bobby tugged Andy out of her seat. "Come on, I'll buy you some lunch."

"We'll talk in a few," Andy said to me, heading with Bobby into the lunch line.

Unbelievable.

I propped my elbows up on the table and plunked my face in my hands, stunned at the unexpected turn of events. This was turning out to be one craaaazy day.

And what was even weirder is that no one was paying Andy and Bobby one bit of attention. They were too busy moaning and groaning over their loss of love to notice the overly happy new couple.

Maya showed up at the table, plopping her lunch on the surface. "Hey, how's it going?"

"Not bad. How are you? Are things getting better at home?"

She shrugged. "I guess so. I finally talked to my parents yesterday and told them they have to back off. I can juggle school and a boyfriend without my grades suffering."

"Good for you!" I was thrilled Maya had finally put her foot down. She did her best to obey her parents' wishes. It wasn't fair for them to treat her this way. "And what did they say?"

"They didn't seem too thrilled, but they let it go. I'm glad they did, because I am *not* giving up on Scott. I'd just sneak out and see him if I needed to." She glanced around. "Hey, where's Andy?"

"She's in line," I said, then paused dramatically. "With Bobby Loward."

"What?" she said, confusion written across her face.

"They're dating now. And they're also going to prom together."

"Whoa, whoa, whoa," she said, holding her hands up. "Back up. When did they start dating?"

I laughed. "I think, like, five minutes ago."

Andy and Bobby returned, carrying their lunch trays.

I let Andy fill Maya in on all the juicy details as I sat back and stayed quiet. Maya squealed and cooed with Andy over her new relationship. This was Andy's time to shine, and I didn't want to butt in.

Besides, I hadn't even matched them up. I guess love was still going on around school, whether I had a hand in it or not. That thought should have been comforting, but it just reminded me of what a bad job I was doing as a cupid.

The lunch bell rang.

I gathered my stuff and went to anthropology class, where more cranky students were griping about the woes of lost love.

By now I was wearing thin. My nerves were raw from hearing so much complaining. I didn't think I could sit through another class like this. I needed a moment to myself in peace and quiet, even if just for a bathroom break.

I borrowed the hall pass from the teacher, claiming I wasn't feeling well and needed to see the nurse, and practically ran to the bathroom. The shuffle-sprint I was doing probably looked ultrastupid, but I needed a quiet moment to collect myself.

I ducked into a stall and sat on the lidded toilet, forcing myself to breathe in calmly through my nose and out my mouth. Maybe it was time to practice some Zen-like relaxation techniques I'd learned from Andy's mom. I closed my eyes and pretended I was on some Tibetan mountain, looking at the sunrise.

A couple of minutes later I felt remarkably calm. There was something to this meditation stuff. I should try it more often. Maybe Andy's mom wasn't so wacky after all.

Okay, I could totally handle this situation. What was important was to keep my focus and come up with a way to repair the matchmaking damage I'd done. Maybe I could take my time and do fewer matches in a day, but make them higher quality. I could stay home in the evenings instead of going out until I'd paired everyone who was unhappy.

Yeah, that part sucked, but this was my job, so there was no sense griping about it. After all, it certainly wasn't going to fix itself. Only one person could make things right—me.

With that in mind, I stood and grabbed the door handle to exit the stall. Then I heard a few voices come into the bathroom . . . one being Mallory's.

I bit back a groan of misery and parked myself back down on the seat. No way did I want yet another confrontation with Her Royal Snottiness.

"Omigod, did you see Mitzi's dress today? Totally tacky," one of the girls said.

"Ew, I know!" another chimed in. I heard lip-smacking sounds—one of them must have been fixing lipstick. "Who wears shoulder pads anymore? That's so eighties."

"Yeah, I guess," Mallory said, her voice sounding a bit flat.

"Well, I'm superhot now. I'm ready to head back out," the first girl said.

"Go ahead, you guys. I'll meet you in a sec. I gotta . . . go to the bathroom," Mallory replied.

I heard the door close.

Great. Trapped in the bathroom with my archenemy, a.k.a. Satan's Future Bride. Just how I wanted to spend my serenity break time.

Suddenly, I heard a sniffling sound. Then a few choked-back sobs that echoed off the tiled walls.

Wow, was she *crying*? I didn't know Mallory had a soul, much less emotions.

It hit me—she must be really upset about James and Mitzi being together. Seeing them around, happy with each other, must be getting under her skin.

Crap, what should I do?

If I came out, she might be embarrassed to be busted crying. But I'd never seen her like this before, and a part of me felt bad for her. Especially since I was the one who'd caused this misery for her through my matchmaking. It didn't matter if she was my nemesis—helping her was my professional obligation.

Well, it was now or never.

I opened the door slowly and peeked my head around the corner. Mallory was slumped over on the edge of the sink, dabbing at her tears with a tissue. I shuffled to the far end of the row of sinks. My movement caught her eye and she gasped, straightening up instantly.

"Geez, you scared me," she said, her lip automatically curling up at the sight of me. "Wait—were you eavesdropping on us?"

I rolled my eyes. "Like I want to listen in on your conversations. There *are* other reasons to go in the bathroom, you know." Not that I was actually using it for that purpose, but she didn't need to know that.

Mallory stood, heading to the door. "Whatever."

Okay, this wasn't going well so far. Maybe not one of my better ideas.

"Look, I'm sorry if you're upset," I said.

She stopped and turned to me slowly. "I'm. Fine," she bit out through ground teeth. "And even if I weren't, I don't need *your* pity."

"You know what?" I retorted, sick of her crap and unable to stop myself, "I never did anything to deserve you treating me like this. I know you think I had a thing for James, but I didn't. I don't need to steal friends' guys."

Especially if that guy was James. Ew.

Her jaw dropped open, and she stared at me for a moment. Then she lifted her chin and glared at me over her nose.

"Whatever," she huffed. "Once you got tired of trying to take my boyfriend, you decided to move on to someone else." She paused and tilted her head, tapping a finger to her chin. "Gee, I wonder if Derek knows how strongly you feel about him. I know you've been crushing on him since freshman year. He's in the cafeteria right now. Maybe he should find out."

Mallory grabbed the door handle and jerked it open, stalking out of the bathroom. Her tall heels clacked across the tiled floor in the hallway.

Heart about to pound out of my chest, I followed right on her heels, my brain desperately clawing around for what to do.

"Stop," I said, my throat choked up. She kept moving.

We burst through the cafeteria doors and reached Derek's table, where he was surrounded by his jock friends and a couple of girls in Mallory's group.

Mallory slid into an open seat. I stopped right beside her. This could *not* be happening.

"Hey, everyone," she said, her eyes wide as she glanced around and caught Derek's attention, "I learned some interesting info about our good friend Felicity. She's in love. And you'll never guess who the guy is."

Chapter 20

Hearing Mallory spill things out like that, so freaking rudely, totally pushed me past my limit. No way was she going to get glory from outing me.

Um, so to speak.

Nope, I'd just have to "out" myself.

Digging my nails into my palms, I said in a loud voice, "Let me spare you the boring story, Mallory." I turned to Derek, who stared at me. "It's you, Derek. I've had a crush on you since freshman year. What can I say? You're a great guy. Who wouldn't want to be with you?"

The whole cafeteria went silent. It seemed everyone was shocked that I'd actually confessed my feelings, out loud, in public.

Even Mallory blinked rapidly, unsure of what to do.

Derek's eyes went wide, and his jaw dropped.

Before he could speak, I charged on, tears welling in my eyes. "But don't worry—I won't throw myself on you."

I dragged in a deep, ragged breath. With blurry vision, I faced Mallory. "You know, I may not be the smartest girl, or the prettiest girl, but at least I can go to bed every night grateful I'm not like you."

With that, I whirled around and fled the cafeteria, not even stopping to apologize to the people I bumped into. I charged down the hallway and ducked into the library—back to the empty room where Derek and I used to meet—then let the tears flow freely.

I cried for a couple of minutes with my back pressed against a bookshelf, my chest aching in embarrassment. God, what an idiot I was! No way could it have worked. He was so out of my league.

And now I was a joke. I'd never hear the end of this, and I was sure news would be all over school within an hour about my dramatic declaration of love. In fact, they were probably laughing their asses off in the cafeteria right now about me.

Well, maybe not Derek—he didn't seem like that kind of guy— but I probably shocked him in a bad, bad way. No way would he still take me to prom, now that our "just friends" agreement was shot.

At any rate, after my little confession, I was going to have to join a convent now. I sniffled loudly and tried to imagine what life as a nun would be like. It would be happy and fun, like the musical *The Sound of Music*. Those nuns were always dancing around on hilltops and singing.

Maybe there was actually something to that idea. No evil people trying to make you look bad. No worries about dating.

But no chance of finding love at all.

No, I'd just have to suck it up out here in the real world and try to make it. Once I got to college, I wouldn't be seeing most of these people anyway.

But I *would* have to see them when I left the sanctuary of the library, and for the rest of this year.

And all of next.

Ugh. I wondered if there was a way to transfer to another school. Or maybe Mom could homeschool me from now on.

I heard a light cough in the room and looked up. Derek stood in the doorway.

I glanced away and swiped at the tears in my eyes, trying

to pretend like I wasn't crying. Like I hadn't spilled my guts in front of everyone in the most mortifying way possible. What had seemed courageous at the time looked really, really stupid in retrospect.

Derek scratched the back of his neck, his eyes intense as they locked with mine. "I need to talk to you."

He looked almost angry. Was he mad because I'd embarrassed him? I hadn't even thought he might be ticked from my public confessional.

We stared at each other for a long, uncomfortable moment. I dropped my gaze. I didn't know what else to say, especially since I'd pretty much laid it all out in the cafeteria.

Then Derek was suddenly right in front of me, touching under my chin to tilt my face up toward him. He brushed my lips with his and then deepened the kiss, his hands stroking my neck and back.

Oh God, is this really happening? Is Derek really kissing me?

Yeah, screw the nun idea—*this* was the stuff I wanted.

I breathed in his light cologne as we continued to kiss. I had no idea how long it lasted, nor did I care. It was everything I'd ever dreamed it would be. His mouth tasted warm and slightly sweet.

He tugged me closer to his body. I wrapped my arms around his neck, falling into this amazing moment.

Derek pulled away, and I fought the urge to drag his head back down to kiss me more.

I bit my lower lip and looked up into his eyes, only inches from mine. "Does this mean you're not pissed at me for the way I . . . blabbed my feelings?"

He cupped my face. "Felicity, I am totally, utterly crazy about you. But I'm also mad that you left like that. You didn't give me a chance to respond."

Shame swirled in my chest. Derek was right—I hadn't even considered that he could possibly match my feelings. I hadn't let him say anything, too afraid he was going to break my heart, right there in front of Mallory and the others.

I squeaked out through a tight throat, "I was embarrassed."

He dropped one hand and pressed it against my back, creating delicious sensations. "I practically did everything I could to show you I fell for you. And you still didn't get it."

Wait—he'd liked me, even before my confession? Wow, I was totally clueless.

No wonder I was such a bad matchmaker. I hadn't seen what

was right in front of my nose. First, Andy and Bobby. And now, this. It was high time I opened my eyes and really looked at what was going on around me.

"Sorry. Apparently, I'm pretty bad at things like this."

Derek laughed. "Yeah, I figured that much out." He pulled back, grabbed my hand, and sat with me at one of the nearby tables. "Look, I have something else to confess to you."

"What's that? You like to collect American Girl dolls or something?" I chuckled.

"Not quite." Derek's eyes darted away from mine, and he swallowed hard, suddenly looking nervous. "Look, I know what you are."

This time, my throat completely closed. I knew beyond a shadow of a doubt that he was talking about the cupid thing.

I stared at him in horror, wondering what to do. I must have given myself away somehow. I was so going to get canned. Janet was going to pitch a fit.

I drew in a deep, calming breath. "What are you talking about?" Yeah, maybe denial was the route to go. I could plead the fifth.

He raised an eyebrow, then dug into his pants pocket and whipped out a hot-pink LoveLine 3000.

Just like mine.

I stared at the PDA for a good thirty seconds, trying to figure out what to say. Pieces fell into place—Derek's hesitation to talk about his job. His continued questions about *my* job. The starry-eyed couples that *I* didn't match up.

He shifted on his chair. "Aren't you going to say anything?"

I opened my mouth, then closed it. Then burst out laughing.

"What a pair we are," I said, wiping more tears off my face. "I never would have guessed you were a cupid. So, why didn't Janet tell me I wasn't the only one here?"

"Well, she'd suddenly decided she wanted a guy and a girl to work each school, since she figured it would be more balanced. So I was hired just a few weeks ago to be our school's other match-maker."

"Then you knew I was a cupid here."

Derek shook his head, a small smile on his face. "Actually, Janet didn't tell me who the other cupid was. She wanted to wait until she'd had a chance to meet with both of us together. But I figured it out when you made the whole school fall for me."

I blushed. "Oh, that."

"When I realized you were one of the only people not touched by the cupid magic, I started watching you closely. I didn't say anything at first because I was trying to find the right way to approach you on how we could fix the . . . hasty matches you made."

"Yeah, that didn't go so hot," I groaned.

He grabbed my hand and rubbed his fingers across the tops of mine. "Don't sweat it. We'll get it fixed, together."

I had a hard time thinking with his warm hands touching me, but I made a valiant attempt anyway. "So no one else knows about us, then?"

"Are you kidding?" Derek scoffed. "Can you imagine the hazing the football team would give me?"

"That's true."

Wow, he was in an even worse spot than I was. And here I kept feeling sorry for myself about keeping it a secret. Poor Derek had to keep looking macho while making his love matches in secret.

With a hot-pink PDA, to top it off.

He snuggled closer to me, his warm side pressing against mine. "Wanna get out of here? You have a class to get back to, and I'd better finish my lunch." He paused. "But we could hang out after art class. Study or grab some coffee or something."

"That sounds great," I said. It would be good to have his help and advice in fixing up the matchmaking disaster. It would be even better to have him to kiss and hang out with as way more than just friends.

Hand in hand, Derek and I strolled out of the library. For the first time in weeks I felt a sense of contentment with life. Andy had found a great match in the unlikely Bobby. Maya had stood up to her parents and was still doing wonderfully with Scott. And I'd finally gotten the guy of my dreams.

Love was all around. What more could a cupid want?

It's not over yet! Check out this sneak peek of the last
book in the Stupid Cupid trilogy:

Pucker Up

Could a person die of happiness overload? Because if that was
possible, I was so going to keel over any second.

But what a way to go.

My brand-new boyfriend Derek's strong, lean fingers threaded
tightly through mine as we strolled through the door of Starbucks.
It was our first official date since we began going out yesterday
afternoon. We'd decided to grab some coffee after school to discuss
how to help all the brokenhearted single people I'd hastily matched
with one another, when I was trying to reverse the effects of me
accidentally making them all fall in love with him.

Yeah, not one of the better ideas I've had in the couple of
months since being hired by my boss, Janet, at Cupid's Hollow.
But fortunately for me, I also found out yesterday that Derek was

a fellow cupid, and he'd promised to help me out. And I just knew that we were going to make things right—together.

"Hey, Felicity, what kind of drink do you want?" he asked, turning those piercing green eyes to me.

I swallowed, wanting to pinch myself in überglee. I was on an honest-to-God date with the guy I'd been crushing on since freshman year, something I'd fantasized about for*ever*.

"Felicity?" he asked, one eyebrow raised.

Hey, dork! He asked you a question! I mentally chided myself, trying to snap out of my love haze.

"Um, how about a mocha Frappucino?" I suggested. "Those are super good." And super laden with caffeine. Yum!

He smiled, his cheek dimpling slightly. "Sure. Why don't you find us a private spot to sit?"

I nodded, picking out a booth in the back corner where no one was around and settling into one side of the table. Plenty of isolation for us to discuss our top-secret cupid business matters.

Digging through my purse, I pulled out my hot-pink LoveLine 3000, the handheld technology we cupids use to send matchmaking emails to our targets. I put it on my lap, turning it on. While I waited for Derek to return, I kept myself occupied by staring at his absolutely perfect butt.

After a couple of minutes, Derek sauntered over to the table, drinks in hand, and slid into the booth seat across from me. I accepted mine gratefully and forced myself to take a slow sip through the straw, not wanting to give myself brain freeze. That crap *hurt*.

"Okay, I'm dying to ask you a question," I finally said, leaning over the table toward Derek in excitement. "When Janet hired you, did she take you to the bow-and-arrow room and give you a . . . demonstration?"

I rubbed the middle of my chest, remembering how it had felt at my interview to have the gold arrow hit me and disappear, leaving only a tingle. Janet, our boss, sure didn't mess around . . . she'd wanted to make sure I knew the cupid powers were real. Not that I'd doubted her after she shot me, but over time, I'd learned the reality of matchmaking all too well . . . both the ups and downs.

Derek laughed. "So she shot you with an arrow also. Glad I wasn't the only doubter she'd hired."

God, it was so awesome to be able to work with my new boyfriend. I'd finally have someone I could talk about my cupid woes with! Not that I wasn't desperate to dish it all to my two best friends, Andy and Maya . . . but my contract specifically stipulated I wasn't allowed to tell anyone the specifics of my job, upon pain of death.

Okay, the contract terms weren't *that* drastic, but I just knew something awful *would* happen to me. I sure didn't want to find out what though.

"Janet's kind of scary," I whispered, almost afraid that by some weird voodoo, she could overhear me talking about her.

"No kidding. She's intimidating." He took the lid off his cup, releasing a puff of steam into the air, and took a drink.

"So, how many matches have you made so far?" I asked him. We each had a weekly quota to meet, and I was eager for tips and motivation.

"Only a few." He shrugged. "I'm trying to take my time and still perfect my profiles. It's hard work, studying everyone and making sure I represent them accurately."

I nodded in sympathy. "Yeah, it took me a while to do those too."

A souring thought hit me, and I pinched my lips together. If I'd taken more time to add greater details to my profiles, like Derek was doing, maybe I wouldn't have made so many bad matches since I'd started working as a cupid. And thus, there wouldn't be so many desolate people grumping their way through school when their love spells had worn off.

Shaking my head resolutely, I pushed the thought out of my brain. All I'd been trying to do was get the school's attention off

Derek and back on one another, where it belonged. Besides, there were now two matchmakers on the job at Greenville High, ready and eager to get things fixed up before prom, which would be in just more than three weeks.

And I couldn't focus on my own prom happiness with Derek until I got these disaster matches resolved, once and for all.

I took my LoveLine 3000 out of my lap and put it on the tabletop, ready to get down to business. "Did you bring yours?"

"Sure did." Derek tugged his out of his back pocket and turned it on. "Last night, I made a list of everyone in school who was currently single and in need of a match. I'll e-mail you half of the list." He bent his head over the PDA, typing on the little keyboard.

Weird, I'd never thought about e-mailing another cupid. I wonder what would happen when he sent me the document. Would it make us fall even more in love? Maybe we would be like my parents were when I'd had a "brilliant" idea and decided to matchmake the two of them for their anniversary a few weeks ago.

I shuddered, remembering their feet sticking out of their bedroom doorway as they went at it on their floor. Time to push that gross little memory into the dark recesses of my brain, back where it belonged.

"Hey, you still here?" Derek asked, a crooked grin on his face.

He reached over and brushed my hand, causing my skin to tingle.

"Yeah, sorry, had a bad flashback," I said, drinking some of my Frappucino with my free hand. I'd tell him about matchmaking my parents later, after I'd done another mental scrub or two or twenty.

My PDA vibrated. I opened my new e-mail from Derek, half expecting my chest to tingle—the surefire identifier of a love match.

Nothing happened.

After staring dumbly at the screen for several long seconds, I almost smacked my own forehead. *Duh, Felicity.* I'd forgotten that cupids can't matchmake themselves, so Derek sending me an e-mail wouldn't have any power over me anyway.

I focused my attention on the list, scrolling down to check out the names. "Okay, I need to make matches for everyone on here, right?"

"Yeah. I think if we take our time and do some quality matches, they should hold together with better odds."

My stomach twitched. He was right, of course, but I was embarrassed that Derek, who had been a cupid only for a few weeks, had managed to figure out more about matchmaking than I did.

He reached back into his pocket and pulled out his cupid manual. "Each person can be matched with someone else on the list, just to keep things simple. I prepared the two lists according to the manual. There was one formula that seemed overly complicated, but the one on page . . . ," he drawled off, flipping through the book, "fifty-two seemed like it would do the job."

Derek turned the manual facing toward me and pointed at a tiny chart, filled with wavy lines and arrows.

Yeahhhhh . . . I'd completely forgotten about that book. Whoops. The writing was so dry and boring, I'd almost fallen asleep reading it. I think I'd stuffed it in my bookshelf a few days after becoming a cupid and never opened it up again, preferring to wing it my own way.

I nodded sagely, pretending I could interpret the chart. "Good thinking. That one should work out great." Right, like I knew what the crap he was talking about.

I made a mental note to dig my manual out again and make a more valiant effort to read the damn thing. Geez, we'd only been here a short time, and already, Derek was schooling me in the art and science of matchmaking. How mortifying.

My cheeks burned.

Well, it was my own fault. This wasn't the time for embarrassment or shame. I had to do what the situation called for, and none of my ideas had worked out well so far. Time to try Derek's plan now.

"Let's run this by Janet first," I said, "just to be safe." I knew from experience that our boss liked to be kept in the loop. Plus, she'd probably like to see us working together. And anything that made Janet happy was good in my book.

"Sure, that's a good idea." He took a draw from his drink and smiled at me. "I'm looking forward to working with you."

"Me too," I replied with a happy sigh, a warm glow spreading through my chest and limbs.

I didn't need a love arrow shot at me to make me get tingles—being in Derek's presence was more than enough.

"Well," Janet said to me and Derek, leaning back in her plush executive chair, "I think that's a great plan. And I like even more how you two are working together on this. I was hoping you'd get along." She gave us a nod of approval.

I beamed, happy that not only could Janet squeeze in a meeting with us on such short notice, but she also approved of our idea on how to fix the matchmaking mess at school. That way, we could get started on it ASAP.

"Thanks," I replied, excitement bubbling in my voice. "Derek's great to work with." With all the strength I could muster, I resisted the urge to cast a lovey-dovey gaze at Derek, who was sitting in the chair beside me, across from Janet's desk. But out of the corner of my eye, I saw him smile at my words.

After solidifying our matchmaking plan at Starbucks earlier today, Derek and I had also decided we'd lie low with the boyfriend/girlfriend stuff around work until we'd scoped the situation out first. Janet didn't know we were dating, and we didn't want to make anything more complicated than necessary right now.

"Okay, let me see your PDAs," she said, reaching her hands out toward us. "I'll download a copy of your lists for reference."

We handed them over to her and, one by one, she synched them to her main computer. After she was done, she laid them on the desk. "I'll review the documents later, but it seems like you're on the right track." She paused. "Actually Derek, since you're here, there's another guy cupid I'd like to introduce you to. He's in the office next door. Felicity, we'll be back in a few minutes—just wait right here."

"Sure thing," I said, trying not to give Derek any inappropriately slutty looks as he filed past me and followed Janet out the door.

I crossed my legs and fidgeted for a couple of minutes. Then, I stood up and plucked my PDA off her desk so I could put it back in my purse. As I lifted the LoveLine 3000, I saw my name at the top of a list on the left page of her daily planner. My heart pounded, and I swallowed hard.

Was I in trouble? Maybe she was on to me and Derek and was upset about us dating. Or maybe she'd found out some of my other cupid secrets, like that I'd previously matchmade my friend Maya with three guys . . . or that I'd paired up my parents for their anniversary. I'd deleted those e-mails from my LoveLine 3000, but maybe she'd gotten the info somehow.

I had to know. With a furtive glance at the door, I quickly jerked the planner off the desk, scanning its contents. It was a to-do list, and there was a checkbox beside me. And after my name was Derek's name. Under us were other pairs of names. What was this?

Then, it hit me.

Janet must have matchmade me and Derek.

My jaw dropped in shock. Janet had paired us up? But I didn't remember getting a love e-mail or anything else yesterday. In fact, I didn't remember any sort of weird tingling feeling at all.

I shook my head, staring at the words. How had she done it?

Well, cupids *have* been around for thousands of years. Maybe there were many other methods of matchmaking that I hadn't even imagined.

The doorknob turned. I dropped the planner, deftly plopping back in my seat. Something told me I probably wasn't supposed to know about being matchmade, so I decided to keep my mouth shut about what I'd seen.

"You can call him anytime," Janet said to Derek as they walked into the room. "Okay, we're all done here, you two." She moved behind her desk and handed Derek his PDA back. "I'll see you in your individual meetings next week."

He turned and smiled at me, his eyes lighting up as they crinkled in the corners. I melted a little, like ooey gooey butter. If he and I were together a hundred years, I'd never get enough of him.

Then, a startling thought flew into my mind. Did this new discovery of mine mean the only reason Derek was in love with me was because we'd been paired together by Janet? Was his love genuine, or just a result of a magically induced spell? I knew mine was sincere, since I'd been in love with him for years. But it wasn't the same story for Derek.

With suddenly shaky legs, I stood, offering Janet a weak smile. "Well, I'd better get home before my mom wonders where her car is."

We headed back to the parking lot. I tucked my hand into Derek's, but on the inside, I was almost dizzy from the new worry that swirled in my head. I knew I should be more understanding of Janet's actions. After all, that's what *I* did for a living—find people who belong together and give them a chance at love. But I had to admit, I'd never considered the idea that Derek and I could have been paired up too.

I guess I'd just figured that he and I were destined to be together, and that my bold confession to him in the cafeteria yesterday about my true feelings had set our destiny into motion. I still couldn't believe I'd found the courage to spill my guts in front of Derek, his friends, and a crapload of people eating lunch, me loudly proclaiming that I'd been crushing on him since freshman year. Even now, my stomach flipped over itself when I thought of it.

About the Author

Rhonda Stapleton started writing a few years ago to appease the voices in her head. She lives in northeast Ohio with her two kids, her manpanion, and their lazy dog. Visit her website at RhondaStapleton.com, or drop her a line at rhonda@rhondastapleton.com.

simonTEEN

Simon & Schuster's **Simon Teen**
e-newsletter delivers current updates on
the hottest titles, exciting sweepstakes, and
exclusive content from your favorite authors.

Visit **TEEN.SimonandSchuster.com** to
sign up, post your thoughts, and find out what
every avid reader is talking about!

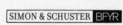

Friendship.
BETRAYAL.
Makeovers.
REVENGE.

And don't miss this other funny read from
Eileen Cook:

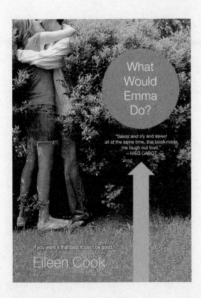

"Sassy and sly and
sweet all at the same time."
—Meg Cabot

• • • • • From Simon Pulse • Published by Simon & Schuster • • • • • •

A promise broken. A secret betrayed.
What do you believe?

"I love this book."
—Lauren Myracle, bestselling author of *ttyl* and *ttfn*

From Simon Pulse
Published by Simon & Schuster

Funny. Fresh. Fabulous.

Don't miss these books by Julie Linker:

From Simon Pulse

Published by Simon & Schuster

www.LiPSMACKER.com

LiP SMACKER®

LOUNGE

Check out
hot new movies
and music

Post
your favorite
pictures

Create
a colorful,
new avatar

Quiz
yourself and
your friends

Tell us what
you think

Share your
creativity

Show off your
Lip Smacker
collection

Explore
ways to start
a collection

Download
popular video
links

Find out the
latest celebrity
buzz

Express your
favorite flavor

at www.lipsmackerlounge.com